KNOPF
75
YEARS·OF·PUBLISHING

Also by Roald Dahl

AUTOBIOGRAPHIES

Going Solo
Boy

NOVEL

My Uncle Oswald

SHORT STORIES

Over to You
Someone Like You
Kiss Kiss
Twenty-Nine Kisses from Roald Dahl
Switch Bitch
Tales of the Unexpected
More Tales of the Unexpected
The Best of Roald Dahl

CHILDREN'S BOOKS

James and the Giant Peach
Charlie and the Chocolate Factory
The Magic Finger
Fantastic Mr. Fox
Charlie and the Great Glass Elevator
Danny, the Champion of the World
The Wonderful Story of Henry Sugar and Six More
The Enormous Crocodile
The Twits
George's Marvellous Medicine
Revolting Rhymes
The BFG
Dirty Beasts
The Witches
Boy
The Giraffe, the Pelly and Me
Matilda
Rhyme Stew

Ah, Sweet Mystery of Life

Ah, Sweet Mystery of Life

STORIES BY

ROALD DAHL

Illustrated by John Lawrence

ALFRED A. KNOPF NEW YORK 1990

THIS IS A BORZOI BOOK

PUBLISHED BY ALFRED A. KNOPF, INC.

 Published in the United States by Alfred A. Knopf, Inc., New York. Distributed by Random House, Inc., New York. Originally published in Great Britain by Michael Joseph Ltd., London, in 1989.

Grateful acknowledgement is made to Alfred A. Knopf, Inc., for permission to reprint "The Ratcatcher," "Rummins," "Mr. Hoddy," and "Mr. Feasey" from *Someone Like You* by Roald Dahl. Copyright 1953 by Roald Dahl. "Parson's Pleasure" and "The Champion of the World" from *Kiss, Kiss* by Roald Dahl. Copyright © 1959 by Roald Dahl. Reprinted by permission of Alfred A. Knopf, Inc.

Library of Congress Cataloguing-in-Publication Data
Dahl, Roald.
Ah, sweet mystery of life: stories / by Roald Dahl.
—1st American ed.
p. cm.
ISBN 0-394-58265-9
I. Title.
PR6054.A35A74 1990
823'.914—dc20 89-43292 CIP

Manufactured in the United States of America
First American Edition

Contents

Preface

IN 1946 the war was over and I was thirty years old. I came back to England then and spent some years living in my mother's house. First we were in Great Missenden, and later we moved a few miles away to the High Street in Old Amersham. This was fine Buckinghamshire country, with its rolling hills and beechwoods and small green fields. I was writing nothing but short stories at that time and I wrote them slowly and carefully at my own pace. In this way, I would complete three or sometimes four of them each year. I worked on nothing else. I was totally preoccupied with the short story, and I would sell the first serial rights of each one when it was finished, either to *The New Yorker* or to some other American magazine like *Collier's* or the *Saturday Evening Post.* Then the second serial rights would go to magazines in other countries, and whenever I had enough stories to make a book, a book it would be.

It was a pleasant leisurely life entailing about four hours' work a day, seven days a week. I enjoyed it and I now realise how fortunate I was in being able to come up with a new plot whenever I needed one. This routine of four hours a day and never any more left me plenty of time for messing around with other things. This messing around very soon took on a particular shape because I met (I have forgotten exactly how or where) a man of my own age called Claud. Claud was married, with two small children, and he lived in a dark and dingy flat in Old Amersham. He worked behind the counter in a butcher's shop in that town and he was not in the least interested in writing. In fact, he had difficulty in composing a sentence of much more than four words. But Claud and I had other things in common.

We both had a passion for gambling in small amounts on horses and greyhounds. As well as that, we shared a love of trying to acquire something by stealth without paying for it. By this I don't mean common or garden thievery. We would never have robbed a house or stolen a bicycle. Ours was the sporting type of stealing. It was poaching pheasants or tickling trout or nicking a few plums from a farmer's orchard. These are practices that are condoned by the right people in the countryside. There is a delicious element of risk in them, especially in the poaching, and a good deal of skill is required.

Claud was an acknowledged expert on such matters and he was proud of it. He taught me everything. His knowledge of the habits of wild animals, be they rats or pheasants or stoats or rabbits or hares, was very great, and he was at his happiest when he was out in the woods in the dead of night. Poaching pheasants and tickling trout and going to the flapping tracks—these were the three things that absorbed and thrilled us most of all.

Flapping tracks are unlicensed greyhound race meetings held in some farmer's field where six dogs chase a stuffed white rabbit which is pulled along on a cord by a man at the far end of the field who is frantically turning the pedals of an upturned bicycle with his hands. These meetings are frequented by gypsies and spivs and all manner of unsavoury characters who bring their dogs to race. Shady bookmakers set up their stands along the side of the hedge and a great deal of betting goes on. This sort of thing was made for a man like Claud. It was also made for me, and it wasn't long before I was buying and breeding my own greyhounds for flapping tracks. Claud and I would train them and at one time I had more than twenty dogs housed in kennels just outside Amersham, and we looked after them together. In spite of the fun of poaching pheasants, I think we probably had more fun plotting and scheming to get a winner at the flapping track than we had with anything else.

The stories in this book all grew out of my experiences with Claud. They were written at the time when we were together, in the late 1940s, and rereading them again now fills me with acute nostalgia and with vivid memories of those sweet days many years ago.

R.D. 1989

Ah, Sweet Mystery of Life

MY COW started bulling at dawn and the noise can drive you crazy if the cowshed is right under your window. So I got dressed early and phoned Claud at the filling station to ask if he'd give me a hand to lead her down the steep hill and across the road over to Rummins's farm to have her serviced by Rummins's famous bull.

Claud arrived five minutes later and we tied a rope around the cow's neck and set off down the lane on this

cool September morning. There were high hedges on either side of the lane and the hazel bushes had clusters of big ripe nuts all over them.

"You ever seen Rummins do a mating?" Claud asked me.

I told him I had never seen anyone do an official mating between a bull and a cow.

"Rummins does it special," Claud said. "There's nobody in the world does a mating the way Rummins does it."

"What's so special about it?"

"You got a treat coming to you," Claud said.

"So has the cow," I said.

"If the rest of the world knew about what Rummins does at a mating," Claud said, "he'd be world famous. It would change the whole science of dairy farming all over the world."

"Why doesn't he tell them then?" I asked.

"I doubt he's ever even thought about it," Claud said. "Rummins isn't one to bother his head about things like that. He's got the best dairy herd for miles around and that's all he cares about. He doesn't want the newspapers swarming all over his place asking questions, which is exactly what would happen if it ever got out."

"Why don't you tell me about it," I said.

We walked on in silence for a while, the cow pulling ahead.

"I'm surprised Rummins said yes to lending you his bull," Claud said. "I've never known him do that before."

At the bottom of the lane we crossed the Aylesbury road and climbed up the hill on the other side of the valley towards the farm. The cow knew there was a bull

up there somewhere and she was pulling harder than ever on the rope. We had to trot to keep up with her.

There were no gates at the farm entrance, just a wide gap and a cobbled yard beyond. Rummins, carrying a pail of milk across the yard, saw us coming. He set the pail down slowly and came over to meet us. "She's ready then, is she?" he said.

"Been yelling her head off," I said.

Rummins walked around my cow, examining her carefully. He was a short man, built squat and broad like a frog. He had a wide frog mouth and broken teeth and shifty eyes, but over the years I had grown to respect him for his wisdom and the sharpness of his mind.

"All right then," he said. "What is it you want, a heifer calf or a bull?"

"Can I choose?"

"Of course you can choose."

"Then I'll have a heifer," I said, keeping a straight face. "We want milk, not beef."

"Hey, Bert!" Rummins called out. "Come and give us a hand!"

Bert emerged from the cowsheds. He was Rummins's youngest son, a tall boneless boy with a runny nose and something wrong with one eye. The eye was pale and misty-grey all over, like a boiled fish eye, and it moved quite independently from the other eye. "Get another rope," Rummins said.

Bert fetched a rope and looped it around my cow's neck, so that she now had two ropes holding her, my own and Bert's. "He wants a heifer," Rummins said. "Face her into the sun."

"Into the sun?" I said. "There isn't any sun."

"There's always sun," Rummins said. "Them bloody clouds don't make no difference. Come on now. Get a jerk on, Bert. Bring her round. Sun's over there."

With Bert holding one rope and Claud and me holding the other, we manoeuvred the cow round until her head was facing directly towards the place in the sky where the sun was hidden behind the clouds.

5

"I told you it was different," Claud whispered. "You're going to see something soon you've never seen in your life before."

"Hold her steady now!" Rummins ordered. "Don't let her jump round!" Then he hurried over to a shed in the far corner of the yard and brought out the bull. He was an enormous beast, a black-and-white Friesian, with short legs and a body like a ten-ton truck. Rummins was leading it by a chain attached to a steel ring through the bull's nose.

"Look at them bangers on him," Claud said. "I'll bet you've never seen a bull with bangers like that before."

"Tremendous," I said. They were like a couple of cantaloupe melons in a carrier bag and they were almost dragging on the ground as the bull waddled forward.

"You better stand back and leave the rope to me," Claud said. "You get right out of the way." I was happy to comply.

The bull approached my cow slowly, staring at her with dangerous white eyes. Then he started snorting and pawing the ground with one foreleg.

"Hang on tight!" Rummins shouted to Bert and Claud. They were leaning back against their respective ropes, holding them very taut and at right angles to the cow.

"Come on, boy," Rummins whispered softly to the bull. "Go to it, lad."

With surprising agility the bull heaved his front part up on to the cow's back and I caught a glimpse of a long scarlet penis, as thin as a rapier and just as stiff, and then it was inside the cow and the cow staggered and the bull heaved and snorted and in thirty seconds it was all over. The bull climbed down again slowly and stood there looking somewhat pleased with himself.

"Some bulls don't know where to put it," Rummins said. "But mine does. Mine could thread a needle with that dick of his."

"Wonderful," I said. "A bull's-eye."

"That's exactly where the word come from," Rummins said. "A bull's-eye. Come on, lad," he said to the bull. "You've had your lot for today." He led the bull back to the shed and shut him in, and when he returned I thanked him, and then I asked him if he really believed that facing the cow into the sun during the mating would produce a female calf.

"Don't be so damn silly," he said. "Of course I believe it. Facts is facts."

"What do you mean facts is facts?"

"I mean what I say, mister. It's a certainty. That's right, ain't it, Bert?"

Bert swivelled his misty eye around in its socket and said, "Too bloody true it's right."

"And if you face her away from the sun does it get you a male?"

"Every single time," Rummins said. I smiled and he saw it. "You don't believe me, do you?"

"Not really," I said.

"Come with me," he said. "And when you see what I'm going to show you, you'll bloody well have to believe me. You two stay here and watch that cow," he said to Claud and Bert. Then he led me into the farmhouse. The room we went into was dark and small and dirty. From a drawer in the sideboard he produced a whole stack of thin exercise books. They were the kind children use at school. "These is calving books," he announced. "And in here is a record of every mating that's ever been done on this farm since I first started thirty-two years ago."

He opened a book at random and allowed me to look. There were four columns on each page: "COW'S NAME," "DATE OF MATING," "DATE OF BIRTH," "SEX OF CALF."

I glanced down the sex column. *Heifer,* it said. *Heifer, Heifer, Heifer, Heifer, Heifer, Heifer.*

"We don't want no bull calves here," Rummins said. "Bull calves is a dead loss on a dairy farm."

I turned over a page. *Heifer,* it said. *Heifer, Heifer, Heifer, Heifer, Heifer.*

"Hey," I said. "Here's a bull calf."

"That's quite right," Rummins said. "Now take a look at what I wrote opposite that one at the time of the mating." I glanced at column two. *Cow jumped round,* it said.

"Some of them gets fractious and you can't hold 'em steady," Rummins said. "So they finish up facing the other way. That's the only time I ever get a bull."

"This is fantastic," I said, leafing through the book.

"Of course it's fantastic," Rummins said. "It's one of the most fantastic things in the whole world. Do you actually know what I average on this farm? I average ninety-eight percent heifers year in, year out! Check it for yourself. Go on and check it. I'm not stopping you."

"I'd like very much to check it," I said. "May I sit down?"

"Help yourself," Rummins said. "I've got work to do." I found a pencil and paper and I proceeded to go through each one of the thirty-two little books with great care. There was one book for each year, from 1915 to 1946. There were approximately eighty calves a year born on the farm, and my final results over the thirty-two-year period were as follows:

Heifer calves	2,516
Bull calves	56
Total calves born, including stillborn	2,572

I went outside to look for Rummins. Claud had disappeared. He'd probably taken my cow home. I found Rummins in the dairy pouring milk into the separator. "Haven't you ever told anyone about this?" I asked him.

"Never have," he said.

"Why not?"

"I reckon it ain't nobody else's business."

"But my dear man, this could transform the entire milk industry the world over."

"It might," he said. "It might easily do that. It wouldn't do the beef business no harm, either, if they could get bulls every time."

"How did you hear about it in the first place?"

"My old dad told me," Rummins said. "When I were about eighteen, my old dad said to me, 'I'll tell you a secret,' he said, 'that'll make you rich.' And he told me this."

"Has it made you rich?"

"I ain't done too bad for myself, have I?" he said.

"But did your father offer any sort of explanation as to why it works?" I asked.

Rummins explored the inner rim of one nostril with the end of his thumb, holding the nose flap between thumb and forefinger as he did so. "A very clever man, my old dad was," he said. "Very clever indeed. Of course he told me how it works."

"How?"

"He explained to me that a cow don't have nothing to do with deciding the sex of the calf," Rummins said. "All a cow's got is an egg. It's the bull decides what the sex is going to be. The sperm of the bull."

"Go on," I said.

"According to my old dad, a bull has two different kinds of sperm, female sperm and male sperm. You follow me so far?"

"Yes," I said. "Keep going."

"So when the old bull shoots off his sperm into the cow, a sort of swimming race takes place between the male and the female sperm to see which one can reach the egg first. If the female sperm wins, you get a heifer."

"But what's the sun got to do with it?" I asked.

"I'm coming to that," he said, "so listen carefully. When an animal is standing on all fours like a cow, and when you face her head into the sun, then the sperm has also got to travel directly into the sun to reach the egg. Switch the cow around and they'll be travelling away from the sun."

"So what you're saying," I said, "is that the sun exerts a pull of some sort on the female sperm and makes them swim faster than the male sperm."

"Exactly!" cried Rummins. "That's exactly it! It exerts a pull! It drags them forward! That's why they always win! And if you turn the cow round the other way, it's pulling them backwards and the male sperm wins instead."

"It's an interesting theory," I said. "But it hardly seems likely that the sun, which is millions of miles away, could exert a pull on a bunch of spermatozoa inside a cow."

"You're talking rubbish!" cried Rummins. "Absolute and utter rubbish! Don't the moon exert a pull on the bloody tides of the ocean to make 'em high and low? Of course it does! So why shouldn't the sun exert a pull on the female sperm?"

"I see your point."

Suddenly, Rummins seemed to have had enough. "You'll have a heifer calf for sure," he said, turning away. "Don't you worry about that."

"Mr. Rummins," I said.

"What?"

"Is there any reason why this shouldn't work with humans as well?"

"Of course it'll work with humans," he said. "Just so long as you remember everything's got to be pointed in the right direction. A cow ain't lying down, you know. It's standing on all fours."

"I see what you mean."

"And it ain't no good doing it at night either," he said, "because the sun is shielded behind the earth and it can't influence anything."

"That's true," I said, "but have you any sort of proof it works with humans?"

Rummins laid his head to one side and gave me another of his long sly broken-toothed grins. "I've got four boys of my own, ain't I?" he said.

"So you have."

"Ruddy girls ain't no use to me around here," he said. "Boys is what you want on a farm and I've got four of 'em, right?"

"Right," I said, "you're absolutely right."

Parson's Pleasure

MR. BOGGIS was driving the car slowly, leaning back comfortably in the seat with one elbow resting on the sill of the open window. How beautiful the countryside, he thought; how pleasant to see a sign or two of summer once again. The primroses especially. And the hawthorn. The hawthorn was exploding white and pink and red along the hedges and the primroses were growing underneath in little clumps, and it was beautiful.

He took one hand off the wheel and lit himself a cigarette. The best thing now, he told himself, would be

to make for the top of Brill Hill. He could see it about half a mile ahead. And that must be the village of Brill, that cluster of cottages among the trees right on the very summit. Excellent. Not many of his Sunday sections had a nice elevation like that to work from.

He drove up the hill and stopped the car just short of the summit on the outskirts of the village. Then he got out and looked around. Down below, the countryside was spread out before him like a huge green carpet. He could see for miles. It was perfect. He took a pad and pencil from his pocket, leaned against the back of the car, and allowed his practised eye to travel slowly over the landscape.

He could see one medium farmhouse over on the right, back in the fields, with a track leading to it from the road. There was another larger one beyond it. There was a house surrounded by tall elms that looked as though it might be a Queen Anne, and there were two likely farms away over on the left. Five places in all. That was about the lot in this direction.

Mr. Boggis drew a rough sketch on his pad showing the position of each so that he'd be able to find them easily when he was down below, then he got back into the car and drove up through the village to the other side of the hill. From there he spotted six more possibles—five farms and one big white Georgian house. He studied the Georgian house through his binoculars. It had a clean prosperous look, and the garden was well ordered. That was a pity. He ruled it out immediately. There was no point in calling on the prosperous.

In this square then, in this section, there were ten possibles in all. Ten was a nice number, Mr. Boggis told himself. Just the right amount for a leisurely afternoon's work. What time was it now? Twelve o'clock. He would have liked a pint of beer in the pub before he started, but on Sundays they didn't open until one. Very well, he would have it later. He glanced at the notes on his pad. He decided to take the Queen Anne first, the house with the elms. It had looked nicely dilapidated through the binoculars. The people there could probably do with some money. He was always lucky with Queen Annes, anyway. Mr. Boggis climbed back into the car, released the hand brake, and began cruising slowly down the hill without the engine.

Apart from the fact that he was at this moment disguised in the uniform of a clergyman, there was nothing very sinister about Mr. Cyril Boggis. By trade he was a dealer in antique furniture, with his own shop and showroom in the King's Road, Chelsea. His premises were not large, and generally he didn't do a great deal of business, but because he always bought cheap, very very cheap, and sold very very dear, he managed to make quite a tidy little income every year. He was a talented salesman, and when buying or selling a piece he could slide smoothly into whichever mood suited the client best. He could become grave and charming for the aged, obsequious for the rich, sober for the godly, masterful for the weak, mischievous for the widow, arch and saucy for the spinster. He was well aware of his gift, using it shamelessly on every possible occasion, and often, at the end of an unusually good performance, it was as much as he could do to prevent himself from turning aside and taking a bow or two as the thundering applause of the audience went rolling through the theatre.

In spite of this rather clownish quality of his, Mr. Boggis was not a fool. In fact, it was said of him by some that he probably knew as much about French, English, and Italian furniture as anyone else in London. He also had surprisingly good taste, and he was quick to recognise and reject an ungraceful design, however genuine the article might be. His real love, naturally, was for the work of the great eighteenth-century English designers, Ince, Mayhew, Chippendale, Robert Adam, Manwaring, Inigo Jones, Hepplewhite, Kent, Johnson, George Smith, Lock, Sheraton, and the rest of them, but even with these he occasionally drew the line. He refused, for example, to allow a single piece from Chippendale's Chinese or Gothic period to come into his showroom, and the same was true of some of the heavier Italian designs of Robert Adam.

During the past few years, Mr. Boggis had achieved considerable fame among his friends in the trade by his ability to produce unusual and often quite rare items with astonishing regularity. Apparently, the man had a source of supply that was almost inexhaustible, a sort of private warehouse, and it seemed that all he had to do was to drive out to it once a week and help himself. Whenever they asked him where he got the stuff, he would smile knowingly and wink and murmur something about a little secret.

The idea behind Mr. Boggis's little secret was a simple one, and it had come to him as a result of something that had happened on a certain Sunday afternoon nearly nine years before, while he was driving in the country.

He had gone out in the morning to visit his old mother, who lived in Sevenoaks, and on the way back the fan belt on his car had broken, causing the engine to overheat and the water to boil away. He had got out of the car and walked to the nearest house, a smallish farm building about fifty yards off the road, and had asked the woman who answered the door if he could please have a jug of water.

While he was waiting for her to fetch it, he happened to glance in through the door to the living room, and there, not five yards from where he was standing, he spotted something that made him so excited the sweat began to come out all over the top of his head. It was a large oak armchair of a type that he had only seen once before in his life. Each arm, as well as the panel at the back, was supported by a row of eight beautifully turned spindles. The back panel itself was decorated by an inlay of the most delicate floral design, and the head of a duck was carved to lie along half the length of either arm. Good God, he thought. This thing is late fifteenth century!

He poked his head in further through the door, and there, by heavens, was another of them on the other side of the fireplace!

He couldn't be sure, but two chairs like that must be worth at least a thousand pounds up in London. And oh, what beauties they were!

When the woman returned, Mr. Boggis introduced himself and straightaway asked if she would like to sell her chairs.

Dear me, she said. But why on earth should she want to sell her chairs?

No reason at all, except that he might be willing to give her a pretty nice price.

And how much would he give? They were definitely

not for sale, but just out of curiosity, just for fun, you know, how much would he give?

Thirty-five pounds.

How much?

Thirty-five pounds.

Dear me, thirty-five pounds. Well, well, that was very interesting. She'd always thought they were valuable. They were very old. They were very comfortable too. She couldn't possibly do without them, not possibly. No, they were not for sale but thank you very much all the same.

They weren't really so very old, Mr. Boggis told her, and they wouldn't be at all easy to sell, but it just happened that he had a client who rather liked that sort of thing. Maybe he could go up another two pounds—call it thirty-seven. How about that?

They bargained for half an hour, and of course in the end Mr. Boggis got the chairs and agreed to pay her something less than a twentieth of their value.

That evening, driving back to London in his old station wagon with the two fabulous chairs tucked away snugly in the back, Mr. Boggis had suddenly been struck by what seemed to him to be a most remarkable idea.

Look here, he said. If there is good stuff in one farmhouse, then why not in others? Why shouldn't he search for it? Why shouldn't he comb the countryside? He could do it on Sundays. In that way, it wouldn't interfere with his work at all. He never knew what to do with his Sundays.

So Mr. Boggis bought maps, large-scale maps, of all the counties around London, and with a fine pen he divided each of them up into a series of squares. Each of these squares covered an actual area of five miles by five, which was about as much territory, he estimated, as he could cope with on a single Sunday, were he to comb it thoroughly. He didn't want the towns and the villages. It was the comparatively isolated places, the large farmhouses and the rather dilapidated country mansions, that he was looking for; and in this way, if he did one square each Sunday, fifty-two squares a year, he would gradually cover every farm and every country house in the home counties.

But obviously there was a bit more to it than that. Country folk are a suspicious lot. So are the impoverished rich. You can't go about ringing their bells and expecting them to show you around their houses just for the asking, because they won't do it. That way you would never get beyond the front door. How then was he to gain admittance? Perhaps it would be best if he didn't let them know he was a dealer at all. He could be a telephone man, the plumber, the gas inspector. He could even be a clergyman. . . .

From this point on, the whole scheme began to take on a more practical aspect. Mr. Boggis ordered a large quantity of superior cards on which the following legend was engraved:

THE REVEREND
CYRIL WINNINGTON BOGGIS

President of the
Society for the Preservation
of Rare Furniture

In association
with The Victoria and
Albert Museum

From now on, every Sunday, he was going to be a nice old parson spending his holiday travelling around on a labour of love for the "Society," compiling an inventory of the treasures that lay hidden in the country homes of England. And who in the world was going to kick him out when they heard that one?

Nobody.

And then, once he was inside, if he happened to spot something he really wanted, well—he knew a hundred different ways of dealing with that.

Rather to Mr. Boggis's surprise, the scheme worked. In fact, the friendliness with which he was received in one house after another through the countryside was, in the beginning, quite embarrassing, even to him. A slice of cold pie, a glass of port, a cup of tea, a basket of plums, even a full sit-down Sunday dinner with the family—such things were constantly being pressed upon him. Sooner or later, of course, there had been some bad moments and a number of unpleasant incidents, but then nine years is more than four hundred Sundays, and that adds up to a great quantity of houses visited. All in all, it had been an interesting, exciting, and lucrative business.

And now it was another Sunday and Mr. Boggis was operating in the county of Buckinghamshire, in one of the most northerly squares on his map, about ten miles from Oxford, and as he drove down the hill and headed for his first house, the dilapidated Queen Anne, he began to get the feeling that this was going to be one of his lucky days.

He parked the car about a hundred yards from the gates and got out to walk the rest of the way. He never liked people to see his car until after a deal was completed. A dear old clergyman and a large station wagon somehow never seemed quite right together. Also the short walk gave him time to examine the property closely from the outside and to assume the mood most likely to be suitable for the occasion.

Mr. Boggis strode briskly up the drive. He was a small fat-legged man with a belly. The face was round and rosy, quite perfect for the part, and the two large brown eyes that bulged out at you from this rosy face gave an impression of gentle imbecility. He was dressed in a black suit with the usual parson's dog collar round his neck, and on his head a soft black hat. He carried an old oak walking stick, which lent him, in his opinion, a rather rustic easygoing air.

He approached the front door and rang the bell. He heard the sound of footsteps in the hall and the door opened and suddenly there stood before him, or, rather, above him, a gigantic woman dressed in riding breeches. Even through the smoke of her cigarette he could smell the powerful odour of stables and horse manure that clung about her.

"Yes?" she asked, looking at him suspiciously. "What is it you want?"

Mr. Boggis, who half expected her to whinny any moment, raised his hat, made a little bow, and handed her his card. "I do apologise for bothering you," he said, and then he waited, watching her face as she read the message.

"I don't understand," she said, handing back the card. "What is it you want?"

Mr. Boggis explained about the Society for the Preservation of Rare Furniture.

"This wouldn't by any chance be something to do with the Socialist Party?" she asked, staring at him fiercely from under a pair of pale bushy brows.

From then on, it was easy. A Tory in riding breeches, male or female, was always a sitting duck for Mr. Boggis. He spent two minutes delivering an impassioned eulogy on the extreme Right Wing Conservative Party, then two more denouncing the Socialists. As a clincher, he made particular reference to the Bill that the Socialists had once introduced for the abolition of blood sports in the country, and went on to inform his listener of his idea of heaven—"though you better not tell the bishop, my dear"—was a place where one could hunt the fox, the stag, and the hare with large packs of tireless hounds from morn till night every day of the week, including Sundays.

Watching her as he spoke, he could see the magic beginning to do its work. The woman was grinning now, showing Mr. Boggis a set of enormous, slightly yellow teeth. "Madam," he cried, "I beg of you, *please* don't get me started on Socialism." At that point, she let out a great guffaw of laughter, raised an enormous red hand, and slapped him so hard on the shoulder that he nearly went over.

"Come in!" she shouted. "I don't know what the hell you want, but come on in!"

Unfortunately, and rather surprisingly, there was nothing of any value in the whole house, and Mr. Boggis, who never wasted time on barren territory, soon made his excuses and took his leave. The whole visit had taken less than fifteen minutes, and that, he told himself as he climbed back into his car and started off for the next place, was exactly as it should be.

From now on, it was all farmhouses, and the nearest was about half a mile up the road. It was a large half-timbered brick building of considerable age, and there was a magnificent pear tree still in blossom covering almost the whole of the south wall.

Mr. Boggis knocked on the door. He waited, but no one came. He knocked again, but still there was no answer, so he wandered around the back to look for the farmer among the cowsheds. There was no one there either. He guessed that they must all still be in church, so he began peering in the windows to see if he could spot anything interesting. There was nothing in the dining room. Nothing in the library either. He tried the next window, the living room, and there, right under his nose, in the little alcove that the window made, he saw a beautiful thing, a semicircular card table in mahogany, richly veneered, and in the style of Hepplewhite, built around 1780.

"Aha," he said aloud, pressing his face hard against glass. "Well done, Boggis."

But that was not all. There was a chair there as well, a single chair, and if he was not mistaken, it was of an even finer quality than the table. Another Hepplewhite, wasn't it? And oh, what a beauty! The lattices on the back were finely carved with the honeysuckle, the husk, and the paterae, the caning on the seat was original, the legs were very gracefully turned, and the two back ones had that peculiar outward splay that meant so much. It was an exquisite chair. "Before this day is done," Mr. Boggis said softly, "I shall have the pleasure of sitting down upon that lovely seat." He never bought a chair without doing this. It was a favourite test of his, and it was always an intriguing sight to see him lowering himself delicately into the seat, waiting for the "give," expertly gauging the precise but infinitesimal degree of shrinkage that the years had caused in the mortice and dovetail joints.

But there was no hurry, he told himself. He would return here later. He had the whole afternoon before him.

The next farm was situated some way back in the fields, and in order to keep his car out of sight, Mr. Boggis had to leave it on the road and walk about six hundred yards along a straight track that led directly into the back yard of the farmhouse. This place, he noticed as he approached, was a good deal smaller than the last, and he didn't hold out much hope for it. It looked rambling and dirty, and some of the sheds were clearly in bad repair.

There were three men standing in a close group in a corner of the yard, and one of them had two large black greyhounds with him, on leashes. When the men caught sight of Mr. Boggis walking forward in his black suit and parson's collar, they stopped talking and seemed suddenly to stiffen and freeze, becoming absolutely still, motionless, three faces turned towards him, watching him suspiciously as he approached.

The oldest of the three was a stumpy man with a wide frog mouth and small shifty eyes, and although Mr. Boggis didn't know it, his name was Rummins and he was the owner of the farm.

The tall youth beside him, who appeared to have

something wrong with one eye, was Bert, the son of Rummins.

The shortish flat-faced man with a narrow corrugated brow and immensely broad shoulders was Claud. Claud had dropped in on Rummins in the hope of getting a piece of pork or ham out of him from the pig that had been killed the day before. Claud knew about the killing—the noise of it had carried far across the fields—and he also knew that a man should have a government permit to do that sort of thing, and that Rummins didn't have one.

"Good afternoon," Mr. Boggis said. "Isn't it a lovely day."

None of the three men moved. At that moment they were all thinking precisely the same thing—that somehow or other this clergyman, who was certainly not the local fellow, had been sent to poke his nose into their business and to report what he found to the government.

"What beautiful dogs," Mr. Boggis said. "I must say I've never been greyhound racing myself, but they tell me it's a fascinating sport."

Again the silence, and Mr. Boggis glanced quickly from Rummins to Bert, then to Claud, then back again to Rummins, and he noticed that each of them had the same peculiar expression on his face, something between a jeer and a challenge, with a contemptuous curl to the mouth, and a sneer around the nose.

"Might I inquire if you are the owner?" Mr. Boggis asked, undaunted, addressing himself to Rummins.

"What is it you want?"

"I do apologise for troubling you, especially on a Sunday."

Mr. Boggis offered his card and Rummins took it and held it up close to his face. The other two didn't move, but their eyes swivelled over to one side, trying to see.

"And what exactly might you be wanting?" Rummins asked.

For the second time that morning, Mr. Boggis explained at some length the aims and ideals of the Society for the Preservation of Rare Furniture.

"We don't have any," Rummins told him when it was over. "You're wasting your time."

"Now, just a minute, sir," Mr. Boggis said, raising a finger. "The last man who said that to me was an old farmer down in Sussex, and when he finally let me into his house, d'you know what I found? A dirty-looking chair in the corner of the kitchen, and it turned out to be worth *four hundred pounds!* I showed him how to sell it, and he bought himself a new tractor with the money."

"What on earth are you talking about?" Claud said. "There ain't no chair in the world worth four hundred pounds."

"Excuse me," Mr. Boggis answered primly, "but there are plenty of chairs in England worth more than twice that figure. And you know where they are? They're tucked away in the farms and cottages all over the country, with the owners using them as steps and ladders and standing on them with hobnailed boots to reach a pot of jam out of the top cupboard or to hang a picture. This is the truth I'm telling you, my friends."

Rummins shifted uneasily on his feet. "You mean to say all you want to do is go inside and stand there in the middle of the room and look around?"

"Exactly," Mr. Boggis said. He was at last beginning to sense what the trouble might be. "I don't want to pry into your cupboards or into your larder. I just want to look at the furniture to see if you happen to have any treasures here, and then I can write about them in our Society magazine."

"You know what I think?" Rummins said, fixing him with his small wicked eyes. "I think you're after buying the stuff yourself. Why else would you be going to all this trouble?"

"Oh, dear me. I only wish I had the money. Of course, if I saw something that I took a great fancy to, and it wasn't beyond my means, I might be tempted to make an offer. But alas, that rarely happens."

"Well," Rummins said, "I don't suppose there's any harm in your taking a look around if that's all you want."

He led the way across the yard to the back door of the farmhouse, and Mr. Boggis followed him; so did the son, Bert, and Claud with his two dogs. They went through the kitchen, where the only furniture was a cheap deal table and a dead chicken lying on it, and they emerged into a fairly large, exceedingly filthy living room.

And there it was! Mr. Boggis saw it at once, and he stopped dead in his tracks and gave a little shrill gasp of shock. Then he stood there for five, ten, fifteen seconds at least, staring like an idiot, unable to believe, not daring to believe what he saw before him. It *couldn't* be true, not possibly! But the longer he stared, the more true it began to seem. After all, there it was standing against the wall right in front of him, as real and as solid as the house itself. And who in the world could possibly make a mistake about a thing like that? Admittedly it was painted white, but that made not the slightest difference. Some idiot had done that. The paint could easily be stripped off. But good God! Just look at it! And in a place like this!

At that point, Mr. Boggis became aware of the three men, Rummins, Bert, and Claud, standing together in a group over by the fireplace, watching him intently. They had seen him stop and gasp and stare, and they must have seen his face turning red, or maybe it was white, but in any event they had seen enough to spoil the whole goddam business if he didn't do something about it quick. In a flash, Mr. Boggis clapped one hand over his heart, staggered to the nearest chair, and collapsed into it, breathing heavily.

"What's the matter with you?" Claud asked.

"It's nothing," he gasped. "I'll be all right in a minute. Please—a glass of water. It's my heart."

Bert fetched him the water, handed it to him, and stayed close beside him, staring down at him with a fatuous leer on his face.

"I thought maybe you were looking at something," Rummins said. The wide frog mouth widened a fraction further into a crafty grin, showing the stubs of several broken teeth.

"No, no," Mr. Boggis said. "Oh, dear me, no. It's just my heart. I'm so sorry. It happens every now and then. But it goes away quite quickly. I'll be all right in a couple of minutes."

He *must* have time to think, he told himself. More important still, he must have time to compose himself thoroughly before he said another word. Take it gently, Boggis. And whatever you do, keep calm. These people may be ignorant, but they are not stupid. They are suspicious and wary and sly. And if it is really true—no, it *can't* be, it *can't* be true . . .

He was holding one hand up over his eyes in a gesture of pain, and now, very carefully, secretly, he made a little crack between two of the fingers and peeked through.

Sure enough, the thing was still there, and on this occasion he took a good long look at it. Yes—he had been right the first time! There wasn't the slightest doubt about it! It was really unbelievable!

What he saw was a piece of furniture that any expert would have given almost anything to acquire. To a layman it might not have appeared particularly impressive, especially when covered over as it was with dirty white paint, but to Mr. Boggis it was a dealer's dream. He knew, as does every other dealer in Europe and America, that among the most celebrated and coveted examples of eighteenth-century English furniture in existence are the three famous pieces known as "the Chippendale Commodes." He knew their history backwards—that the first was "discovered" in 1920, in a house at Moreton-on-the-Marsh, and was sold at Sotheby's the same year; that the other two turned up in the same auction rooms a year later, both coming out of Rainham Hall, Norfolk. They all fetched enormous prices. He couldn't quite remember the exact figure for the first one, or even the second, but he knew for certain that the last one to be sold had fetched thirty-nine hundred guineas. And that was in 1921! Today the same piece would surely be worth ten thousand pounds. Some man, Mr. Boggis couldn't remember his name, had made a study of these commodes fairly recently and had proved that all three must have come from the same workshop, for the veneers were all from the same log, and the same set of templates had been used in the construction of each. No invoices had been found for any of them, but all the experts were agreed that these three commodes could have been executed only by Thomas Chippendale himself, with his own hands, at the most exalted period in his career.

And here, Mr. Boggis kept telling himself as he peered cautiously through the crack in his fingers, here was the fourth Chippendale Commode! And *he* had found it! He would be rich! He would also be famous. Each of the other three was known throughout the furniture world by a special name—the Chastleton Commode, the First Rainham Commode, the Second Rainham Commode. This one would go down in history as the Boggis Commode! Just imagine the faces of the boys up there in London when they got a look at it tomorrow morning!

And the luscious offers coming in from the big fellows over in the West End—Frank Partridge, Mallett, Jetley, and the rest of them! There would be a picture of it in the *Times*, and it would say, "The very fine Chippendale Commode which was recently discovered by Mr. Cyril Boggis, a London dealer . . ." Dear God, what a stir he was going to make!

This one here, Mr. Boggis thought, was almost exactly similar to the Second Rainham Commode. (All three, the Chastleton and the two Rainhams, differed from one another in a number of small ways.) It was a most impressive handsome affair built in the French rococo style of Chippendale's Director period, a kind of large fat chest of drawers set upon four carved and fluted legs that raised it about a foot from the ground. There were six drawers in all, two long ones in the middle and two shorter ones on either side. The serpentine front was magnificently ornamented along the top and sides and bottom, and also vertically between each set of drawers, with intricate carvings of festoons and scrolls and clusters. The brass handles, although partly obscured by white paint, appeared to be superb. It was, of course, a rather "heavy" piece, but the design had been executed with such elegance and grace that the heaviness was in no way offensive.

"How're you feeling now?" Mr. Boggis heard someone saying.

"Thank you, thank you, I'm much better already. It passes quickly. My doctor says it's nothing to worry about really, so long as I rest for a few minutes whenever it happens. Ah yes," he said, raising himself slowly to his feet. "That's better. I'm all right now."

A trifle unsteadily, he began to move around the room examining the furniture, one piece at a time, commenting upon it briefly. He could see at once that apart from the commode it was a very poor lot.

"Nice oak table," he said. "But I'm afraid it's not old enough to be of any interest. Good comfortable chairs, but quite modern, yes, quite modern. Now this cupboard, well, it's rather attractive, but again, not valuable. This chest of drawers"—he walked casually past the Chippendale Commode and gave it a little contemptuous flip with his fingers—"worth a few pounds, I daresay, but no more. A rather crude reproduction, I'm afraid. Probably made in Victorian times. Did you paint it white?"

"Yes," Rummins said. "Bert did it."

"A very wise move. It's considerably less offensive in white."

"That's a strong piece of furniture," Rummins said. "Some nice carving on it too."

"Machine-carved," Mr. Boggis answered superbly, bending down to examine the exquisite craftsmanship. "You can tell it a mile off. But still, I suppose it's quite pretty in its way. It has its points."

He began to saunter off, then he checked himself and turned slowly back again. He placed the tip of one finger against the point of his chin, laid his head over to one side, and frowned as though deep in thought.

"You know what?" he said, looking at the commode, speaking so casually that his voice kept trailing off. "I've just remembered . . . I've been wanting a set of legs something like that for a long time. I've got a rather curious table in my own little home, one of those low things that people put in front of the sofa, sort of coffee table, and last Michaelmas, when I moved house, the foolish movers damaged the legs in the most shocking way. I'm very fond of that table. I always keep my big Bible on it, and all my sermon notes."

He paused, stroking his chin with the finger. "Now I was just thinking. These legs on your chest of drawers might be very suitable. Yes, they might indeed. They could easily be cut off and fixed on to my table."

He looked around and saw the three men standing absolutely still, watching him suspiciously, three pairs of eyes, all different but equally mistrusting, small pig eyes for Rummins, large slow eyes for Claud, and two odd eyes for Bert, one of them very queer, and boiled and misty pale, with a little black dot in the centre, like a fish eye on a plate.

Mr. Boggis smiled and shook his head. "Come, come, what on earth am I saying? I'm talking as though I owned the piece myself. I do apologise."

"What you mean to say is you'd like to buy it," Rummins said.

"Well . . ." Mr. Boggis glanced back at the commode, frowning. "I'm not sure. I might . . . and then again . . . on second thoughts . . . no . . . I think it might be a bit too much trouble. It's not worth it. I'd better leave it."

"How much were you thinking of offering?" Rummins asked.

"Not much, I'm afraid. You see, this is not a genuine antique. It's merely a reproduction."

"I'm not so sure about that," Rummins told him. "It's been in *here* over twenty years, and before that it was up at the Manor House. I bought it there myself at auction when the old Squire died. You can't tell me that thing's new."

"It's not exactly new, but it's certainly not more than about sixty years old."

"It's more than that," Rummins said. "Bert, where's that bit of paper you once found at the back of one of them drawers? That old bill."

The boy looked vacantly at his father.

Mr. Boggis opened his mouth, then quickly shut it again without uttering a sound. He was beginning literally to shake with excitement, and to calm himself he walked over to the window and stared out at a plump brown hen pecking around for stray grains of corn in the yard.

"It was in the back of that drawer underneath all them rabbit snares," Rummins was saying. "Go on and fetch it out and show it to the parson."

When Bert went forward to the commode, Mr. Boggis turned round again. He couldn't stand not watching him. He saw him pull out one of the big middle drawers, and he noticed the beautiful smooth way in which the drawer slid open. He saw Bert's hand dipping inside and rummaging around among a lot of wires and strings.

"You mean this?" Bert lifted out a piece of folded yellowing paper and carried it over to the father, who unfolded it and held it up close to his face.

"You can't tell me this writing ain't bloody old," Rummins said, and he held the paper out to Mr. Boggis, whose whole arm was shaking as he took it. It was brittle and it crackled slightly between his fingers. The writing was in a long sloping copperplate hand:

Edward Montagu, Esq.

Dr.
To Thos. Chippendale

A large mahogany Commode Table of exceeding fine wood, very rich carvd, set upon fluted legs, two very neat shapd long drawers in the middle part and two ditto on each side, with rich chasd Brass Handles and Ornaments, the whole compleatly finishd in the most exquisite taste . . . £87

Mr. Boggis was holding on to himself tight and fighting to suppress the excitement that was spinning round inside him and making him dizzy. Oh God, it was wonderful! With the invoice, the value had climbed even higher. What in heaven's name would it fetch now? Twelve thousand pounds? Fourteen? Maybe fifteen or even twenty? Who knows?

Oh, boy!

He tossed the paper contemptuously onto the table and said quietly, "It's exactly what I told you, a Victorian reproduction. This is simply the invoice that the seller—the man who made it and passed it off as an antique—gave to his client. I've seen lots of them. You'll notice that he doesn't say he made it himself. That would give the game away."

"Say what you like," Rummins announced, "but that's an old piece of paper."

"Of course it is, my dear friend. It's Victorian, late Victorian. About 1890. Sixty or seventy years old. I've seen hundreds of them. That was a time when masses of cabinetmakers did nothing else but apply themselves to faking the fine furniture of the century before."

"Listen, Parson," Rummins said, pointing at him with a thick dirty finger, "I'm not saying as how you may not know a fair bit about this furniture business, but what I *am* saying is this. How on earth can you be so mighty sure it's a fake when you haven't even seen what it looks like underneath all that paint?"

"Come here," Mr. Boggis said. "Come over here and I'll show you." He stood beside the commode and waited for them to gather round. "Now, anyone got a knife?"

Claud produced a horn-handled pocketknife, and Mr. Boggis took it and opened the smallest blade. Then, working with apparent casualness but actually with extreme care, he began chipping off the white paint from a small area on the top of the commode. The paint flaked away cleanly from the old hard varnish underneath, and when he had cleared away about three square inches, he stepped back and said, "Now, take a look at that!"

It was beautiful—a warm little patch of mahogany, glowing like a topaz, rich and dark with the true colour of its two hundred years.

"What's wrong with it?" Rummins asked.

"It's processed! Anyone can see that!"

"How can you see it, mister? You tell us."

"Well, I must say that's a trifle difficult to explain. It's chiefly a matter of experience. My experience tells me that without the slightest doubt this wood has been processed with lime. That's what they use for mahogany, to give it that dark aged colour. For oak, they use potash salts, and for walnut it's nitric acid, but for mahogany it's always lime."

The three men moved a little closer to peer at the wood. There was a slight stirring of interest among them now.

It was always intriguing to hear about some new form of crookery or deception.

"Look closely at the grain. You see that touch of orange in among the dark red-brown. That's the sign of lime."

They leaned forward, their noses close to the wood, first Rummins, then Claud, then Bert.

"And then there's the patina," Mr. Boggis continued.

"The what?"

He explained to them the meaning of this word as applied to furniture.

"My dear friends, you've no idea the trouble these rascals will go to to imitate the hard beautiful bronze-like appearance of genuine patina. It's terrible, really terrible, and it makes me quite sick to speak of it!" He was spitting each word sharply off the tip of the tongue and making a sour mouth to show his extreme distaste. The men waited, hoping for more secrets.

"The time and trouble that some mortals will go to in order to deceive the innocent!" Mr. Boggis cried. "It's perfectly disgusting! D'you know what they did here, my friends? I can recognise it clearly. I can almost *see* them doing it, the long, complicated ritual of rubbing the wood with linseed oil, coating it over with French polish that has been cunningly coloured, brushing it down with pumice stone and oil, beeswaxing it with a wax that contains dirt and dust, and finally giving it the heat treatment to crack the polish so that it looks like two-hundred-year-old varnish! It really upsets me to contemplate such knavery!"

The three men continued to gaze at the little patch of dark wood.

"Feel it!" Mr. Boggis ordered. "Put your fingers on it! There, how does it feel, warm or cold?"

"Feels cold," Rummins said.

"Exactly, my friend! It happens to be a fact that faked patina is always cold to the touch. Real patina has a curiously warm feel to it."

"This feels normal," Rummins said, ready to argue.

"No, sir, it's cold. But of course it takes an experienced and sensitive fingertip to pass a positive judgment. You couldn't really be expected to judge this any more than I could be expected to judge the quality of your barley. Everything in life, my dear sir, is experience."

The men were staring at this queer moonfaced clergyman with the bulging eyes, not quite so suspiciously now because he did seem to know a bit about his subject. But they were still a long way from trusting him.

Mr. Boggis bent down and pointed to one of the metal drawer handles on the commode. "This is another place where the fakers go to work," he said. "Old brass normally has a colour and character all of its own. Did you know that?"

They stared at him, hoping for still more secrets.

"But the trouble is that they've become exceedingly skilled at matching it. In fact, it's almost impossible to tell the difference between 'genuine old' and 'faked old.' I don't mind admitting that it has me guessing. So there's not really any point in our scraping the paint off these handles. We wouldn't be any the wiser."

"How can you possibly make new brass look like old?" Claud said. "Brass doesn't rust, you know."

"You are quite right, my friend. But these scoundrels have their own secret methods."

"Such as what?" Claud asked. Any information of this nature was valuable, in his opinion. One never knew when it might come in handy.

"All they have to do," Mr. Boggis said, "is to place these handles overnight in a box of mahogany shavings saturated in sal ammoniac. The sal ammoniac turns the metal green, but if you rub off the green, you will find underneath it a fine soft silvery-warm lustre, a lustre identical to that which comes with very old brass. Oh, it is so bestial, the things they do! With iron they have another trick."

"What do they do with iron?" Claud asked, fascinated.

"Iron's easy," Mr. Boggis said. "Iron locks and plates and hinges are simply buried in common salt and they come out all rusted and pitted in no time."

"All right," Rummins said. "So you admit you can't tell about the handles. For all you know, they may be hundreds and hundreds of years old, correct?"

"Ah," Mr. Boggis whispered, fixing Rummins with two big bulging brown eyes. "That's where you're wrong. Watch this."

From his jacket pocket, he took out a small screwdriver. At the same time, although none of them saw him do it, he also took out a little brass screw, which he kept well hidden in the palm of his hand. Then he selected one of the screws in the commode—there were four to each handle—and began carefully scraping all traces of white paint from its head. When he had done this, he started slowly to unscrew it.

"If this is a genuine old brass screw from the eighteenth century," he was saying, "the spiral will be slightly uneven and you'll be able to see quite easily that it has been hand-cut with a file. But if this brasswork is faked from more recent times, Victorian or later, then obviously the screw will be of the same period. It will be a mass-produced, machine-made article. Anyone can recognise a machine-made screw. Well, we shall see."

It was not difficult, as he put his hands over the old screw and drew it out, for Mr. Boggis to substitute the new one hidden in his palm. This was another little trick of his, and through the years it had proved a most rewarding one. The pockets of his clergyman's jacket were always stocked with a quantity of cheap brass screws of various sizes.

"There you are," he said, handing the modern screw to Rummins. "Take a look at that. Notice the exact evenness of the spiral? See it? Of course you do. It's just a cheap common little screw that you yourself could buy today in any ironmonger's in the country."

The screw was handed round from the one to the other, each examining it carefully. Even Rummins was impressed now.

Mr. Boggis put the screwdriver back into his pocket, together with the fine hand-cut screw that he'd taken from the commode, and then he turned and walked slowly past the three men towards the door.

"My dear friends," he said, pausing at the entrance to the kitchen, "it was so good of you to let me peep inside your little home—so kind. I do hope I haven't been a terrible old bore."

Rummins glanced up from examining the screw. "You didn't tell us what you were going to offer," he said.

"Ah," Mr. Boggis said. "That's quite right, I didn't, did I? Well, to tell you the honest truth, I think it's all a bit too much trouble. I think I'll leave it."

"How much would you give?"

"You mean that you really wish to part with it?"

"I didn't say I wished to part with it. I asked you how much."

Mr. Boggis looked across at the commode, and he laid his head first to one side, then to the other, and he frowned, and pushed out his lips, and shrugged his shoulders, and gave a little scornful wave of the hand as though to say the thing was hardly worth thinking about really, was it?

"Shall we say . . . ten pounds. I think that would be fair."

"Ten pounds!" Rummins cried. "Don't be so ridiculous, Parson, *please!*"

"It's worth more'n that for firewood!" Claud said, disgusted.

"Look here at the bill!" Rummins went on, stabbing that precious document so fiercely with his dirty forefinger that Mr. Boggis became alarmed. "It tells you exactly what it cost! Eighty-seven pounds! And that's when it was new. Now it's antique, it's worth double!"

"If you'll pardon me, no, sir, it's not. It's a secondhand reproduction. But I'll tell you what, my friend—I'm being rather reckless, I can't help it—I'll go up as high as fifteen pounds. How's that?"

"Make it fifty," Rummins said.

A delicious little quiver like needles ran all the way down the back of Mr. Boggis's legs and then under the soles of his feet. He had it now. It was his. No question

about that. But the habit of buying cheap, as cheap as it was humanly possible to buy, acquired by years of necessity and practice, was too strong in him now to permit him to give in so easily.

"My dear man," he whispered softly, "I only *want* the legs. Possibly I could find some use for the drawers later on, but the rest of it, the carcass itself, as your friend so rightly said, it's firewood, that's all."

"Make it thirty-five," Rummins said.

"I *couldn't*, sir, I *couldn't!* It's not worth it. And I simply mustn't allow myself to haggle like this about a price. It's all wrong. I'll make you one final offer, and then I must go. Twenty pounds."

"I'll take it," Rummins snapped. "It's yours."

"Oh dear," Mr. Boggis said, clasping his hands. "There I go again. I should never have started this in the first place."

"You can't back out now, Parson. A deal's a deal."

"Yes, yes, I know."

"How're you going to take it?"

"Well, let me see. Perhaps if I were to drive my car up into the yard, you gentlemen would be kind enough to help me load it?"

"In a car? This thing'll never go in a car! You'll need a truck for this!"

"I don't think so. Anyway, we'll see. My car's on the road. I'll be back in a jiffy. We'll manage it somehow, I'm sure."

Mr. Boggis walked out into the yard and through the gate and then down the long track that led across the field towards the road. He found himself giggling quite uncontrollably, and there was a feeling inside him as though hundreds and hundreds of tiny bubbles were rising up from his stomach and bursting merrily in the top of his head, like sparkling water. All the buttercups in the field were suddenly turning into golden sovereigns, glistening in the sunlight. The ground was littered with them, and he swung off the track onto the grass so that he could walk among them and tread on them and hear the little metallic tinkle they made as he kicked them around with his toes. He was finding it difficult to stop himself from breaking into a run. But clergymen never run; they walk slowly. Walk slowly, Boggis. Keep calm, Boggis. There's no hurry now. The commode is yours! Yours for twenty pounds, and it's worth fifteen or twenty thousand! The Boggis Commode! In ten minutes it'll be loaded into your car—it'll go in easily—and you'll be driving back to London and singing all the way! Mr. Boggis driving the Boggis Commode home in the Boggis car. Historic occasion. What *wouldn't* a newspaperman give to get a picture of that! Should he arrange it? Perhaps he should.

Wait and see. Oh, glorious day! Oh, lovely sunny summer day! Oh, glory be!

Back in the farmhouse, Rummins was saying, "Fancy that old bastard giving twenty pound for a load of junk like this."

"You did very nicely, Mr. Rummins," Claud told him. "You think he'll pay you?"

"We don't put it in the car till he do."

"And what if it won't go in the car?" Claud asked. "You know what I think, Mr. Rummins? You want my honest opinion? I think the bloody thing's too big to go in the car. And then what happens? Then he's going to say to hell with it and just drive off without it and you'll never see him again. Nor the money either. He didn't seem all that keen on having it, you know."

Rummins paused to consider this new and rather alarming prospect.

"How can a thing like that possibly go in a car?" Claud went on relentlessly. "A parson never has a big car anyway. You ever seen a parson with a big car, Mr. Rummins?"

"Can't say I have."

"Exactly! And now listen to me. I've got an idea. He told us, didn't he, that it was only the legs he was wanting. Right? So all we've got to do is to cut 'em off quick right here on the spot before he comes back, then it'll be sure to go in the car. All we're doing is saving him the trouble of cutting them off himself when he gets home. How about it, Mr. Rummins?" Claud's flat bovine face glimmered with a mawkish pride.

"It's not such a bad idea at that," Rummins said, looking at the commode. "In fact, it's a bloody good idea.

Come on then, we'll have to hurry. You and Bert carry it out into the yard. I'll get the saw. Take the drawers out first."

Within a couple of minutes, Claud and Bert had carried the commode outside and had laid it upside down in the yard amidst the chicken droppings and cow dung and mud. In the distance, halfway across the field, they could see a small black figure striding along the path towards the road. They paused to watch. There was something rather comical about the way in which this figure was conducting itself. Every now and again it would break into a trot, then it did a kind of hop, skip, and jump, and once it seemed as though the sound of a cheerful song came rippling faintly to them from across the meadow.

"I reckon he's balmy," Claud said, and Bert grinned darkly, rolling his misty eye slowly round in its socket.

Rummins came waddling over from the shed, squat and froglike, carrying a long saw. Claud took the saw away from him and went to work.

"Cut 'em close," Rummins said. "Don't forget he's going to use 'em on another table."

The mahogany was hard and very dry, and as Claud worked, a fine red dust sprayed out from the edge of the saw and fell softly to the ground. One by one, the legs came off, and when they were all severed, Bert stooped down and arranged them carefully in a row.

Claud stepped back to survey the results of his labour. There was a longish pause.

"Just let me ask you one question, Mr. Rummins," he said slowly. "Even now, could *you* put that enormous thing into the back of a car?"

"Not unless it was a van."

"Correct!" Claud cried. "And parsons don't have vans, you know. All they've got usually is piddling little Morris Eights or Austin Sevens."

"The legs is all he wants," Rummins said. "If the rest of it won't go in, then he can leave it. He can't complain. He's got the legs."

"Now you know better'n that, Mr. Rummins," Claud said patiently. "You know damn well he's going to start knocking the price if he don't get every single bit of this into the car. A parson's just as cunning as the rest of 'em when it comes to money, don't you make any mistake about that. Especially this old boy. So why don't we give him his firewood now and be done with it. Where d'you keep the axe?"

"I reckon that's fair enough," Rummins said. "Bert, go fetch the axe."

Bert went into the shed and fetched a tall woodcutter's axe and gave it to Claud. Claud spat on the palms of his hands and rubbed them together. Then, with a long-armed high-swinging action, he began fiercely attacking the legless carcass of the commode.

It was hard work, and it took several minutes before he had the whole thing more or less smashed into pieces.

"I'll tell you one thing," he said, straightening up, wiping his brow. "That was a bloody good carpenter put this job together and I don't care what the parson says."

"We're just in time!" Rummins called out. "Here he comes!"

The Ratcatcher

IN THE afternoon the ratcatcher came to the filling station. He came sidling up the driveway with a stealthy, soft-treading gait, making no noise at all with his feet on the gravel. He had an army knapsack slung over one shoulder and he was wearing an old-fashioned black jacket with large pockets. His brown corduroy trousers

were tied around the knees with pieces of white string.

"Yes?" Claud asked, knowing very well who he was.

"Rodent operative." His small dark eyes moved swiftly over the premises.

"The ratcatcher?"

"That's me."

The man was lean and brown with a sharp face and two long sulphur-coloured teeth that protruded from the upper jaw, overlapping the lower lip, pressing it inward. The ears were thin and pointed and set far back on the head, near the nape of the neck. The eyes were almost black, but when they looked at you there was a flash of yellow somewhere inside them.

"You've come very quick."

"Special orders from the Health Officer."

"And now you're going to catch all the rats?"

"Yep."

The kind of dark furtive eyes he had were those of an animal that lives its life peering out cautiously and forever from a hole in the ground.

"How are you going to catch 'em?"

"Ah-h-h," the ratman said darkly. "That's all accordin' to where they is."

"Trap 'em, I suppose."

"Trap 'em!" he cried, disgusted. "You won't catch many rats that way! Rats isn't rabbits you know."

He held his face up high, sniffing the air with a nose that twitched perceptibly from side to side.

"No," he said, scornfully. "Trappin's no way to catch a rat. Rats is clever, let me tell you that. If you want to catch 'em, you got to know 'em. You got to know rats on this job."

I could see Claud staring at him with a certain fascination.

"They're more clever'n dogs, rats is."

"Get away."

"You know what they do? They watch you! All the time you're goin' round preparin' to catch 'em, they're sitting quietly in dark places, watchin' you." The man crouched, stretching his stringy neck far forward.

"So what do you do?" Claud asked, fascinated.

"Ah! That's it, you see. That's where you got to know rats."

"How d'you catch 'em?"

"There's ways," the ratman said, leering. "There's various ways."

He paused, nodding his repulsive head sagely up and

down. "It's all dependin'," he said, "on where they is. This ain't a sewer job, is it?"

"No, it's not a sewer job."

"Tricky thing, sewer jobs. Yes," he said, delicately sniffing the air to the left of him with his mobile nose end, "sewer jobs is very tricky things."

"Not especially, I shouldn't think."

"Oho. You shouldn't, shouldn't you! Well, I'd like to see *you* do a sewer job! Just exactly how would *you* set about it, I'd like to know?"

"Nothing to it. I'd just poison 'em, that's all."

"And where exactly would you put the poison, might I ask?"

"Down the sewer. Where the hell you think I put it!"

"There!" the ratman cried, triumphant. "I knew it! Down the sewer! And you know what'd happen then? Get washed away, that's all. Sewer's like a river, y'know."

"That's what *you* say," Claud answered. "That's only what *you* say."

"It's facts."

"All right then, all right. So what would *you* do, Mr. Know All?"

"That's exactly where you got to know rats, on a sewer job."

"Come on then, let's have it."

"Now listen. I'll tell you." The ratman advanced a step closer; his voice became secretive and confidential, the voice of a man divulging fabulous professional secrets. "You works on the understandin' that a rat is a gnawin' animal, see. Rats *gnaws*. Anything you give 'em, don't matter what it is, anything new they never seen before, and what do they do? They *gnaws* it. So now! There you are! You got a sewer job on your hands. And what d'you do?"

His voice had the soft throaty sound of a croaking frog, and he seemed to speak all his words with an immense wet-lipped relish, as though they tasted good on the tongue. The accent was similar to Claud's, the broad soft accent of the Buckinghamshire countryside, but his voice was more throaty, the words more fruity in his mouth.

"All you do is you go down the sewer and you take along some ordinary paper bags, just ordinary brown paper bags, and these bags is filled with plaster-of-Paris powder. Nothin' else. Then you suspend the bags from the roof of the sewer so they hang down not quite touchin' the water. See? Not quite touchin', and just high enough so a rat can reach 'em."

Claud was listening, rapt.

"There you are, y'see. Old rat comes swimmin' along the sewer and sees the bag. He stops. He takes a sniff at it and it don't smell so bad, anyway. So what's he do then?"

"He *gnaws* it," Claud cried, delighted.

"There! That's it! That's exackly it! He starts *gnawin'* away at the bag and the bag breaks and the old rat gets a mouthful of powder for his pains."

"Well?"

"That does him."

"What? Kills him?"

"Yep. Kills him stony!"

"Plaster of Paris ain't poisonous, you know."

"Ah! There you are! That's exackly where you're wrong, see. This powder swells. When you wet it, it swells. Gets into the rat's tubes and swells right up and kills him quicker'n anythin' in the world."

"*No!*"

"That's where you got to know rats."

The ratman's face glowed with a stealthy pride, and he rubbed his stringy fingers together, holding the hands up close to the face. Claud watched him, fascinated.

"Now—where's them rats?" The word "rats" came out of his mouth soft and throaty, with a rich fruity relish as though he were gargling with melted butter. "Let's take a look at them *rraats.*"

"Over there in the hayrick across the road."

"Not in the house?" he asked, obviously disappointed.

"No. Only around the hayrick. Nowhere else."

"I'll wager they're in the house too. Like as not gettin' in all your food in the night and spreadin' disease and sickness. You got any disease here?" he asked, looking first at me, then at Claud.

"Everyone fine here."

"Quite sure?"

"Oh yes."

"You never know, you see. You could be sickenin' for it weeks and weeks and not feel it. Then all of a sudden—bang!—and it's got you. That's why Dr. Arbuthnot's so particular. That's why he sent me out so quick, see. To stop the spreadin' of disease."

He had now taken upon himself the mantle of the Health Officer. A most important rat he was now, deeply disappointed that we were not suffering from bubonic plague.

"I feel fine," Claud said nervously.

The ratman searched his face again, but said nothing.

"And how are you goin' to catch 'em in the hayrick?"

The ratman grinned, a crafty toothy grin. He reached down into his knapsack and withdrew a large tin, which he held up level with his face. He peered around one side of it at Claud.

"Poison!" he whispered. But he pronounced it "pye-zn," making it into a soft dark dangerous word. "Deadly pye-zn, that's what this is!" He was weighing the tin up and down in his hands as he spoke. "Enough here to kill a million men!"

"Terrifying," Claud said.

"Exackly it! They'd put you inside for six months if they caught you with even a spoonful of this," he said, wetting his lips with his tongue. He had a habit of craning his head forward on his neck as he spoke.

"Want to see?" he asked, taking a penny from his pocket, prising open the lid. "There now! There it is!" He spoke fondly, almost lovingly of the stuff, and he held it forward for Claud to look.

"Corn? Or barley is it?"

"It's oats. Soaked in deadly pye-zn. You take just one of them grains in your mouth and you'd be a gonner in five minutes!"

"Honest?"

"Yep. Never out of me sight, this tin."

He caressed it with his hands and gave it a little shake so that the oat grains rustled softly inside.

"But not today. Your rats don't get this today. They wouldn't have it, anyway. That they wouldn't. There's where you got to know rats. Rats is suspicious. Terrible suspicious, rats is. So today they gets some nice clean tasty oats as'll do 'em no harm in the world. Fatten 'em, that's all it'll do. And tomorrow they gets the same again. And it'll taste so good there'll be all the rats in the districk comin' along after a couple of days."

"Rather clever."

"You got to be clever on this job. You got to be cleverer'n a rat and that's sayin' somethin'."

"You've almost got to be a rat yourself," I said. It slipped out in error, before I had time to stop myself, and I couldn't really help it because I was looking at the man at the time. But the effect upon him was surprising.

"There!" he cried. "Now you got it! Now you really said somethin'! A good ratter's got to be more like a rat than anythin' else in the world! Cleverer even than a rat, and that's not an easy thing to be, let me tell you."

"Quite sure it's not."

"All right then, let's go. I haven't got all day, you know. There's Lady Leonora Benson asking for me urgent up there at the Manor."

"She got rats, too?"

"Everybody's got rats," the ratman said, and he ambled off down the driveway, across the road to the hayrick, and we watched him go. The way he walked was so like a rat it made you wonder—that slow, almost delicate ambling walk with a lot of give at the knees and no sound at all from the footsteps on the gravel. He hopped nimbly over the gate into the field, then walked quickly round the hayrick scattering handfuls of oats on to the ground.

The next day he returned and repeated the procedure.

The day after that he came again, and this time he put down the poisoned oats. But he didn't scatter these; he placed them carefully in little piles at each corner of the rick.

"You got a dog?" he asked when he came back across the road on the third day, after putting down the poison.

"Yes."

"Now if you want to see your dog die an 'orrible twistin' death, all you got to do is let him in that gate sometime."

"We'll take care," Claud told him. "Don't you worry about that."

The next day he returned once more, this time to collect the dead.

"You got an old sack?" he asked. "Most likely we goin' to need a sack to put 'em in."

He was puffed up and important now, the black eyes gleaming with pride. He was about to display the sensational results of his craft to the audience.

Claud fetched a sack and the three of us walked across the road, the ratman leading. Claud and I leaned over the gate, watching. The ratman prowled around the hayrick, bending over to inspect his little piles of poison.

"Somethin' wrong here," he muttered. His voice was soft and angry.

He ambled over to another pile and got down on his knees to examine it closely.

"Somethin' bloody wrong here."

"What's the matter?"

He didn't answer, but it was clear that the rats hadn't touched his bait.

"These are very clever rats here," I said.

"Exactly what I told him, Gordon. These aren't just no ordinary kind of rats you're dealing with here."

The ratman walked over to the gate. He was very annoyed and showed it on his face and around the nose and by the way the two yellow teeth were pressing down into the skin of his lower lip. "Don't give me that crap," he said, looking at me. "There's nothin' wrong with these rats except somebody's feedin' 'em. They got somethin' juicy to eat somewhere and plenty of it. There's no rats in the world'll turn down oats unless their bellies is full to burstin'."

"They're clever," Claud said.

The man turned away, disgusted. He knelt down again and began to scoop up the poisoned oats with a small shovel, tipping them carefully back into the tin. When he had done, all three of us walked back across the road.

The ratman stood near the petrol pumps, a rather sorry, humble ratman now whose face was beginning to take on a brooding aspect. He had withdrawn into himself and was brooding in silence over his failure, the eyes veiled and wicked, the little tongue darting out to one side of the two yellow teeth, keeping the lips moist. It appeared to be essential that the lips should be kept moist. He looked up at me, a quick surreptitious glance, then over at Claud. His nose end twitched, sniffing the air. He raised himself up and down a few times on his toes, swaying gently, and in a voice soft and secretive he said, "Want to see somethin'?" He was obviously trying to retrieve his reputation.

"What?"

"Want to see somethin' *amazin'?*" As he said this, he put his right hand into the deep poacher's pocket of his jacket and brought out a large live rat clasped tight between his fingers.

"Good God!"

"Ah! That's it, y'see!" He was crouching slightly now and craning his neck forward and leering at us and holding this enormous brown rat in his hand, one finger and thumb making a tight circle around the creature's neck, clamping its head rigid so it couldn't turn and bite.

"D'you usually carry rats around in your pockets?"

"Always got a rat or two about me somewhere."

With that he put his free hand into the other pocket and produced a small white ferret.

"Ferret," he said, holding it up by the neck.

The ferret seemed to know him and stayed still in his grasp.

"There's nothin'll kill a rat quicker'n a ferret. And there's nothin' a rat's more frightened of, either."

He brought his hands close together in front of him so that the ferret's nose was within six inches of the rat's face. The pink beady eyes of the ferret stared at the rat. The rat struggled, trying to edge away from the killer.

"Now," he said. "Watch!"

His khaki shirt was open at the neck and he lifted the rat and slipped it down inside his shirt, next to his skin. As soon as his hand was free, he unbuttoned his jacket at the front so that the audience could see the bulge the body of the rat made under his shirt. His belt prevented it from going down lower than his waist.

Then he slipped the ferret in after the rat.

Immediately there was a great commotion inside the shirt. It appeared that the rat was running around the man's body, being chased by the ferret. Six or seven times they went around, the small bulge chasing the larger one, gaining on it slightly each circuit and drawing closer and closer, until at last the two bulges seemed to come together and there was a scuffle and a series of shrill shrieks.

Throughout this performance the ratman had stood absolutely still with legs apart, arms hanging loosely, the dark eyes resting on Claud's face. Now he reached one hand down into his shirt and pulled out the ferret; with the other he took out the dead rat. There were traces of blood around the white muzzle of the ferret.

"Not sure I liked that very much."

"You never seen anythin' like it before, I'll bet you that."

"Can't really say I have."

"Like as not you'll get yourself a nasty little nip in the guts one of these days," Claud told him. But he was clearly impressed, and the ratman was becoming cocky again.

"Want to see somethin' far more *amazin'n* that?" he asked. "You want to see somethin' you'd never even *believe* unless you seen it with your own eyes?"

"Well?"

We were standing in the driveway out in front of the pumps and it was one of those pleasant warm November mornings. Two cars pulled in for petrol, one right after the other, and Claud went over and gave them what they wanted.

"You want to see?" the ratman asked.

I glanced at Claud, slightly apprehensive. "Yes," Claud said. "Come on then, let's see."

The ratman slipped the dead rat back into one pocket, the ferret into the other. Then he reached down into his knapsack and produced—if you please—a second live rat.

"Good Christ!" Claud said.

"Always got one or two rats about me somewhere," the man announced calmly. "You got to know rats on this job, and if you want to know 'em you got to have 'em round you. This is a sewer rat, this is. An old sewer rat, clever as buggery. See him watchin' me all the time, wonderin' what I'm goin' to do? See him?"

"Very unpleasant."

"What are you going to do?" I asked. I had a feeling I was going to like this one even less than the last.

"Fetch me a piece of string."

Claud fetched him a piece of string.

With his left hand, the man looped the string around one of the rat's hind legs. The rat struggled, trying to turn its head to see what was going on, but he held it tight around the neck with finger and thumb.

"Now!" he said, looking about him. "You got a table inside?"

"We don't want the rat inside the house," I said.

"Well—I need a table. Or somethin' flat like a table."

"What about the bonnet of that car?" Claud said.

We walked over to the car and the man put the old sewer rat on the bonnet. He attached the string to the windshield wiper so that the rat was now tethered.

At first it crouched, unmoving and suspicious, a big-bodied grey rat with bright black eyes and a scaly tail that lay in a long curl upon the car's bonnet. It was looking away from the ratman, but watching him sideways to see what he was going to do. The man stepped back a few paces and immediately the rat relaxed. It sat up on its haunches and began to lick the grey fur on its chest. Then it scratched its muzzle with both front paws. It seemed quite unconcerned about the three men standing nearby.

"Now—how about a little bet?" the ratman asked.
"We don't bet," I said.
"Just for fun. It's more fun if you bet."
"What d'you want to bet on?"
"I'll bet you I can kill that rat without usin' my hands. I'll put my hands in my pockets and not use 'em."
"You'll kick it with your feet," Claud said.
It was apparent that the ratman was out to earn some money. I looked at the rat that was going to be killed and began to feel slightly sick, not so much because it was going to be killed but because it was going to be killed in a special way, with a considerable degree of relish.
"No," the ratman said. "No feet."
"Nor arms?" Claud asked.
"Nor arms. Nor legs, nor hands neither."
"You'll sit on it."
"No. No squashin'."
"Let's see you do it."
"You bet me first. Bet me a quid."

"Don't be so bloody daft," Claud said. "Why should we give you a quid?"

"What'll you bet?"

"Nothin'."

"All right. Then it's no go."

He made as if to untie the string from the windshield wiper.

"I'll bet you a shilling," Claud told him. The sick gastric sensation in my stomach was increasing, but there was an awful magnetism about this business and I found myself quite unable to walk away or even move.

"You too?"

"No," I said.

"What's the matter with you?" the ratman asked.

"I just don't want to bet you, that's all."

"So you want me to do this for a lousy shillin'?"

"I don't want you to do it."

"Where's the money?" he said to Claud.

Claud put a shilling piece on the bonnet, near the radiator. The ratman produced two sixpences and laid them beside Claud's money. As he stretched out his hand to do this, the rat cringed, drawing its head back and flattening itself against the bonnet.

"Bet's on," the ratman said.

Claud and I stepped back a few paces. The ratman stepped forward. He put his hands in his pockets and inclined his body from the waist so that his face was on a level with the rat, about three feet away.

His eyes caught the eyes of the rat and held them. The rat was crouching, very tense, sensing extreme danger, but not yet frightened. The way it crouched, it seemed to me it was preparing to spring forward at the man's face;

but there must have been some power in the ratman's eyes that prevented it from doing this, and subdued it, and then gradually frightened it so that it began to back away, dragging its body backwards with slow crouching steps until the string tautened on its hind leg. It tried to struggle back further against the string, jerking its leg to free it. The man leaned forward towards the rat, following it with his face, watching it all the time with his eyes, and suddenly the rat panicked and leaped sideways in the air. The string pulled it up with a jerk that must almost have dislocated its leg.

It crouched again, in the middle of the bonnet, as far away as the string would allow, and it was properly frightened now, whiskers quivering, the long grey body tense with fear.

At this point, the ratman again began to move his face closer. Very slowly he did it, so slowly there wasn't really any movement to be seen at all except that the face just happened to be a fraction closer each time you looked. He never took his eyes from the rat. The tension was considerable and I wanted suddenly to cry out and tell him to stop. I wanted him to stop because it was making me feel sick inside, but I couldn't bring myself to say the word. Something extremely unpleasant was about to happen—I was sure of that. Something sinister and cruel and ratlike, and perhaps it really would make me sick. But I had to see it now.

The ratman's face was about eighteen inches from the rat. Twelve inches. Then ten, or perhaps it was eight, and soon there was not more than the length of a man's hand separating their faces. The rat was pressing its body flat against the car bonnet, tense and terrified. The ratman was also tense, but with a dangerous active tensity that was like a tight-wound spring. The shadow of a smile flickered around the skin of his mouth.

Then suddenly he struck.

He struck as a snake strikes, darting his head forward with one swift knifelike stroke that originated in the muscles of the lower body, and I had a momentary glimpse of his mouth opening very wide and two yellow teeth and the whole face contorted by the effort of mouth-opening.

More than that I did not care to see. I closed my eyes, and when I opened them again the rat was dead and the ratman was slipping the money into his pocket and spitting to clear his mouth.

"That's what they makes lickerish out of," he said. "Rat's blood is what the big factories and the chocolate people use to make lickerish."

Again the relish, the wet-lipped, lip-smacking relish as he spoke the words, the throaty richness of his voice and the thick syrupy way he pronounced the word "lickerish."

"No," he said, "there's nothin' wrong with a drop of rat's blood."

"Don't talk so absolutely disgusting," Claud told him.

"Ah! But that's it, you see. You eaten it many a time. Penny sticks and lickerish bootlaces is all made from rat's blood."

"We don't want to hear about it, thank you."

"Boiled up, it is, in great cauldrons, bubblin' and steamin' and men stirrin' it with long poles. That's one of the big secrets of the chocolate-makin' factories, and no one knows about it—no one except the ratters supplyin' the stuff."

Suddenly he noticed that his audience was no longer with him, that our faces were hostile and sick-looking and crimson with anger and disgust. He stopped abruptly, and without another word he turned and sloped off down the driveway out onto the road, moving with the slow, almost delicate ambling walk that was like a rat prowling, making no noise with his footsteps even on the gravel of the driveway.

Rummins

THE SUN was up over the hills now and the mist had cleared and it was wonderful to be striding along the road with the dog in the early morning, especially when it was autumn, with the leaves changing to gold and yellow and sometimes one of them breaking away and falling slowly, turning slowly over in the air, dropping noiselessly right in front of him onto the grass beside the road. There was a small wind up above, and he could hear the beeches rustling and murmuring like a crowd of people.

This was always the best time of the day for Claud Cubbage. He gazed approvingly at the rippling velvety hindquarters of the greyhound trotting in front of him.

"Jackie," he called softly. "Hey, Jackson. How you feeling, boy?"

The dog half turned at the sound of its name and gave a quick acknowledging wag of the tail.

There would never be another dog like this Jackie, he told himself. How beautiful the slim streamlining, the small pointed head, the yellow eyes, the black mobile nose. Beautiful the long neck, the way the deep brisket curved back and up out of sight into no stomach at all. See how he walked up on his toes, noiselessly, hardly touching the surface of the road at all.

"Jackson," he said. "Good old Jackson."

In the distance, Claud could see Rummins's farmhouse, small, narrow, and ancient, standing back behind the hedge on the right-hand side.

I'll turn round here, he decided. That'll be enough for today.

Rummins, carrying a pail of milk across the yard, saw him coming down the road. He set the pail down slowly and came forward to the gate, leaning both arms on the topmost bar, waiting.

"Morning, Mr. Rummins," Claud said. It was necessary to be polite to Rummins because of eggs.

Rummins nodded and leaned over the gate, looking critically at the dog.

"Looks well," he said.

"He is well."

"When's he running?"

"I don't know, Mr. Rummins."

"Come on. When's he running?"

"He's only ten months yet, Mr. Rummins. He's not even schooled properly, honest."

The small beady eyes of Rummins peered suspiciously over the top of the gate. "I wouldn't mind betting a couple of quid you're having it off with him somewhere secret soon."

Claud moved his feet uncomfortably on the black road surface. He disliked very much this man with the wide frog mouth, the broken teeth, the shifty eyes; and most of all he disliked having to be polite to him because of eggs.

"That hayrick of yours opposite," he said, searching desperately for another subject. "It's full of rats."

"All hayrick's got rats."

"Not like this one. Matter of fact, we've been having a touch of trouble with the authorities about that."

Rummins glanced up sharply. He didn't like trouble with the authorities. Any man who sells eggs black market and kills pigs without a permit is wise to avoid contact with that sort of people.

"What kind of trouble?"

"They sent the ratcatcher along."

"You mean just for a few rats?"

"A few! Blimey, it's *swarming!*"

"Never."

"Honest it is, Mr. Rummins. There's hundreds of 'em."

"Didn't the ratcatcher catch 'em?"

"No."

"Why?"

"I reckon they're too artful."

Rummins began thoughtfully to explore the inner rim of one nostril with the end of his thumb, holding the nose flap between thumb and finger as he did so.

"I wouldn't give thank-you for no ratcatchers," he said. "Ratcatchers is government men working for the soddin' government and I wouldn't give thank-you for 'em."

"Nor me, Mr. Rummins. All ratcatchers is slimy cunning creatures."

"Well," Rummins said, sliding fingers under his cap to scratch the head. "I was coming over soon anyway to fetch in that rick. Reckon I might just as well do it today as any other time. I don't want no government men nosing around my stuff, thank you very much."

"Exactly, Mr. Rummins."

"We'll be over later—Bert and me." With that, he turned and ambled off across the yard.

Around three in the afternoon, Rummins and Bert were seen riding slowly up the road in a cart drawn by a

ponderous and magnificent black cart horse. Opposite the filling station the cart turned off into the field and stopped near the hayrick.

"This ought to be worth seeing," I said. "Get the gun."

Claud fetched the rifle and slipped a cartridge into the breech.

I strolled across the road and leaned against the open gate. Rummins was on the top of the rick now and cutting away at the cord that bound the thatching. Bert remained in the cart, fingering a four-foot-long knife.

Bert had something wrong with one eye. It was pale grey all over, like a boiled fish eye, and although it was motionless in its socket it appeared always to be looking at you and following you round, the way the eyes of the people in some of those portraits do in the museums. Wherever you stood and wherever Bert was looking, there was this faulty eye fixing you sideways with a cold stare, boiled and misty pale with a little black dot in the centre, like a fish eye on a plate.

In his build he was the opposite of his father, who was short and squat like a frog. Bert was a tall, reedy, boneless boy, loose at the joints, even the head loose upon the shoulders, falling sideways as though perhaps it was too heavy for the neck.

"You only made this rick last June," I said to him. "Why take it away so soon?"

"Dad wants it."

"Funny time to cut a new rick, November."

"Dad wants it," Bert repeated, and both his eyes, the sound one and the other, stared down at me with a look of absolute vacuity.

"Going to all that trouble stacking it and thatching it and then pulling it down five months later."

"Dad wants it." Bert's nose was running and he kept wiping it with the back of his hand and wiping the back of the hand on his trousers.

"Come on, Bert," Rummins called, and the boy climbed up on to the rick and stood in the place where the thatch had been removed. He took the knife and began to cut down into the tight-packed hay with an easy-swinging, sawing movement, holding the handle with both hands and rocking his body like a man sawing wood with a big saw. I could hear the crisp cutting noise of the blade against the dry hay and the noise becoming softer as the knife sank deeper into the rick.

"Claud's going to take a pot at the rats as they come out."

The man and the boy stopped abruptly and looked across the road at Claud, who was leaning against the red pump with rifle in hand.

"Tell him to put that bloody rifle away," Rummins said.

"He's a good shot. He won't hit you."

"No one's potting no rats alongside of me, don't matter how good they are."

"You'll insult him."

"Tell him to put it away," Rummins said, slow and hostile. "I don't mind dogs nor sticks but I'll be buggered if I'll have rifles."

The two on the hayrick watched while Claud did as he was told; then they resumed their work in silence. Soon Bert came down into the cart and, reaching out with both hands, he pulled a slice of solid hay away from the rick so that it dropped neatly into the cart beside him.

A rat, grey-black, with a long tail, came out of the base of the rick and ran into the hedge.

"A rat," I said.

"Kill it," Rummins said. "Why don't you get a stick and kill it?"

The alarm had been given now and the rats were coming out quicker, one or two of them every minute, fat and long-bodied, crouching close to the ground as they ran through the grass into the hedge. Whenever the horse saw one of them, it twitched its ears and followed it with uneasy rolling eyes.

Bert had climbed back on top of the rick and was cutting out another bale. Watching him, I saw him suddenly stop, hesitate for perhaps a second, then again begin to cut, but very cautiously this time; and now I could hear a different sound, a muffled rasping noise as the blade of the knife grated against something hard.

Bert pulled out the knife and examined the blade, testing it with his thumb. He put it back, letting it down gingerly into the cut, feeling gently downward until it came again upon the hard object; and once more, when he made another cautious little sawing movement, there came that grating sound.

Rummins turned his head and looked over his shoulder at the boy. He was in the act of lifting an armful of loosened thatch, bending forward with both hands grasping the straw, but he stopped dead in the middle of what he was doing and looked at Bert. Bert remained still, hands holding the handle of the knife, a look of bewilderment on his face. Behind, the sky was a pale clear blue, and the two figures up there on the hayrick stood out sharp and black like an etching against the paleness.

Then Rummins's voice, louder than usual, edged with an unmistakable apprehension that the loudness did nothing to conceal: "Some of them haymakers is too bloody careless what they put on a rick these days."

He paused, and again the silence, the men motionless, and across the road Claud leaning motionless against the red pump. It was so quiet suddenly we could hear a woman's voice far down the valley on the next farm calling the men to food.

Then Rummins again, shouting where there was no

need to shout: "Go on then! Go on an' cut through it, Bert! A little stick of wood won't hurt the soddin' knife!"

For some reason, as though perhaps scenting trouble, Claud came strolling across the road and joined me leaning on the gate. He didn't say anything, but both of us seemed to know that there was something disturbing about these two men, about the stillness that surrounded them and especially about Rummins himself. Rummins was frightened. Bert was frightened too. And now as I watched them, I became conscious of a small vague image moving just below the surface of my memory. I tried desperately to reach back and grasp it. Once I almost touched it, but it slipped away and when I went after it I found myself travelling back and back through many weeks, back into the yellow days of summer—the warm wind blowing down the valley from the south, the big beech trees heavy with their foliage, the fields turning to gold, the harvesting, the haymaking, the rick—the building of the rick.

Instantly, I felt a fine electricity of fear running over the skin of my stomach.

Yes—the building of the rick. When was it we had built it? June? That was it, of course—a hot muggy day in June, with the clouds low overhead and the air thick with the smell of thunder.

And Rummins had said, "Let's for God's sake get it in quick before the rain comes."

And Ole Jimmy had said, "There ain't going to be no rain. And there ain't no hurry either. You know very well when thunder's in the south it don't cross over into the valley."

Rummins, standing up in the cart handing out the

pitchforks, had not answered him. He was in a furious brooding temper because of his anxiety about getting in the hay before it rained.

"There ain't goin' to be no rain before evenin'," Ole Jimmy had repeated, looking at Rummins, and Rummins had stared back at him, the eyes glimmering with a slow anger.

All through the morning we had worked without a pause, loading the hay into the cart, trundling it across the field, pitching it out onto the slowly growing rick that stood over by the gate opposite the filling station. We could hear the thunder in the south as it came toward us and moved away again. Then it seemed to return and remain stationary somewhere beyond the hills, rumbling intermittently. When we looked up, we could see the clouds overhead moving and changing shape in the turbulence of the upper air; but on the ground it was hot and muggy and there was no breath of wind. We worked slowly, listlessly in the heat, shirts wet with sweat, faces shining.

Claud and I had worked beside Rummins on the rick itself, helping to shape it, and I could remember how very hot it had been and the flies around my face and the sweat pouring out everywhere; and especially I could remember the grim scowling presence of Rummins beside me, working with a desperate urgency and watching the sky and shouting at the men to hurry.

At noon, in spite of Rummins, we had knocked off for lunch.

Claud and I had sat down under the hedge with Ole Jimmy and another man, called Wilson, who was a soldier home on leave, and it was too hot to do much talking. Wilson had some bread and cheese and a canteen of cold tea. Ole Jimmy had a satchel that was an old gas-mask container, and in this, closely packed, standing upright with their necks protruding, were six pint bottles of beer.

"Come on," he said, offering a bottle to each of us.

"I'd like to buy one from you," Claud said, knowing very well the old man had little money.

"Take it."

"I must pay you."

"Don't be so daft. Drink it."

He was a very good old man, good and clean, with a clean pink face that he shaved each day. He had used to be a carpenter, but they retired him at the age of seventy and that was some years before. Then the Village Council, seeing him still active, had given him the job of looking after the newly built children's playground, of maintaining the swings and seesaws in good repair, and also of acting as a kind of gentle watchdog, seeing that none of the kids hurt themselves or did anything foolish.

That was a fine job for an old man to have and everybody seemed pleased with the way things were going—until a certain Saturday night. That night Ole Jimmy had got drunk and gone reeling and singing down the middle of the High Street with such a howling noise that people got out of their beds to see what was going on below. The next morning they had sacked him, saying he was a bum and a drunkard not fit to associate with young children on the playground.

But then an astonishing thing happened. The first day that he stayed away—a Monday it was—not one single child came near the playground.

Nor the next day, nor the one after that.

All week the swings and the seesaws and the high slide with steps going up to it stood deserted. Not a child went near them. Instead they followed Ole Jimmy out into a field behind the Rectory and played their games there with him watching; and the result of all this was that after a while the Council had had no alternative but to give the old man back his job.

He still had it now and he still got drunk, and no one said anything about it anymore. He left it only for a few days each year, at haymaking time. All his life Ole Jimmy had loved to go haymaking and he wasn't going to give it up yet.

"You want one?" he asked now, holding a bottle out to Wilson, the soldier.

"No thanks. I got tea."

"They say tea's good on a hot day."

"It is. Beer makes me sleepy."

"If you like," I said to Ole Jimmy, "we could walk across to the filling station and I'll do you a couple of nice sandwiches? Would you like that?"

"Beer's plenty. There's more food in one bottle of beer, me lad, than twenty sandwiches."

He smiled at me, showing two rows of pale-pink, toothless gums, but it was a pleasant smile and there was nothing repulsive about the way the gums showed.

We sat for a while in silence. The soldier finished his bread and cheese and lay back on the ground, tilting his hat forward over his face. Ole Jimmy had drunk three bottles of beer, and now he offered the last to Claud and me.

"No thanks."

"No thanks. One's plenty for me."

The old man shrugged, unscrewed the stopper, tilted his head back and drank, pouring the beer into his mouth with the lips held open so the liquid ran smoothly without gurgling down his throat. He wore a hat that was of no colour at all and of no shape, and it did not fall off when he tilted back his head.

"Ain't Rummins goin' to give that old horse a drink?" he asked, lowering the bottle, looking across the field at the great cart horse that stood steaming between the shafts of the cart.

"Not Rummins."

"Horses is thirsty, just the same as us." Ole Jimmy paused, still looking at the horse. "You got a bucket of water in that place of yours there?"

"Of course."

"No reason why we shouldn't give the old horse a drink then, is there?"

"That's a very good idea. We'll give him a drink."

Claud and I both stood up and began walking towards the gate, and I remember turning and calling back to the old man, "You quite sure you wouldn't like me to bring you a nice sandwich? Won't take a second to make."

He shook his head and waved the bottle at us and said something about taking himself a little nap. We went on through the gate over the road to the filling station.

I suppose we stayed away for about an hour attending to customers and getting ourselves something to eat, and when at length we returned, Claud carrying the bucket of water, I noticed that the rick was at least six feet high.

"Some water for the old horse," Claud said, looking hard at Rummins, who was up in the cart pitching hay on to the rick.

The horse put its head in the bucket, sucking and blowing gratefully at the water.

"Where's Ole Jimmy?" I asked. We wanted the old man to see the water because it had been his idea.

When I asked the question, there was a moment, a brief moment when Rummins hesitated, pitchfork in midair, looking around him.

"I brought him a sandwich," I added.

"Bloody old fool drunk too much beer and gone off home to sleep," Rummins said.

I strolled along the hedge back to the place where we had been sitting with Ole Jimmy. The five empty bottles were lying there in the grass. So was the satchel. I picked up the satchel and carried it back to Rummins.

"I don't think Ole Jimmy's gone home, Mr. Rummins," I said, holding up the satchel by the long shoulder band. Rummins glanced at it but made no reply. He was in a frenzy of haste now because the thunder was closer, the clouds blacker, the heat more oppressive than ever.

Carrying the satchel, I started back to the filling station where I remained for the rest of the afternoon, serving customers. Towards evening, when the rain came, I glanced across the road and noticed that they had got the hay in and were laying a tarpaulin over the rick.

In a few days the thatcher arrived and took the tarpaulin off and made a roof of straw instead. He was a good thatcher and he made a fine roof with long straw, thick and well packed. The slope was nicely angled, the edges cleanly clipped, and it was a pleasure to look at it from the road or from the door of the filling station.

All this came flooding back to me now as clearly as if it were yesterday—the building of the rick on that hot thundery day in June, the yellow field, the sweet woody smell of the hay; and Wilson the soldier, with tennis shoes on his feet, Bert with the boiled eye, Ole Jimmy with the clean old face, the pink naked gums, and Rummins, the broad dwarf, standing up in the cart scowling at the sky because he was anxious about the rain.

At this very moment, there he was again, this Rummins, crouching on top of the rick with a sheaf of thatch in his arms looking round at the son, the tall Bert, motionless also, both of them black like silhouettes against the sky, and once again I felt the fine electricity of fear as it came and went in little waves over the skin of my stomach.

"Go on and cut through it, Bert," Rummins said, speaking loudly.

Bert put pressure on the big knife and there was a high grating noise as the edge of the blade sawed across something hard. It was clear from Bert's face that he did not like what he was doing.

It took several minutes before the knife was through—then again, at last, the softer sound of the blade slicing the tight-packed hay and Bert's face turned sideways to the father, grinning with relief, nodding inanely.

"Go on and cut it out," Rummins said, and still he did not move.

Bert made a second vertical cut the same depth as the first; then he got down and pulled the bale of hay so it came away cleanly from the rest of the rick like a chunk of cake, dropping into the cart at his feet.

Instantly, the boy seemed to freeze, staring stupidly at the newly exposed face of the rick, unable to believe or perhaps refusing to believe what this thing was that he had cut in two.

Rummins, who knew very well what it was, had turned away and was climbing quickly down the other side of the rick. He moved so fast he was through the gate and halfway across the road before Bert started to scream.

Mr. Hoddy

THEY GOT out of the car and went in the front door of Mr. Hoddy's house.

"I've an idea Dad's going to question you rather sharp tonight," Clarice whispered.

"About what, Clarice?"

"The usual stuff. Jobs and things like that. And whether you can support me in a fitting way."

"Jackie's going to do that," Claud said. "When Jackie wins, there won't even be any need for any jobs—"

"Don't you ever mention Jackie to my dad, Claud Cubbage, or that'll be the end of it. If there's one thing in the world he can't abide, it's greyhounds. Don't you ever forget that."

"Oh Christ," Claud said.

"Tell him something else—anything—anything to make him happy, see?" And with that she led Claud into the parlour.

Mr. Hoddy was a widower, a man with a prim sour mouth and an expression of eternal disapproval all over his face. He had the small, close-together teeth of his daughter Clarice, the same suspicious, inward look about the eyes, but none of her freshness and vitality, none of her warmth. He was a small sour apple of a man, grey-skinned and shrivelled, with a dozen or so surviving strands of black hair pasted across the dome of his bald head. But a very superior man was Mr. Hoddy, a grocer's assistant, one who wore a spotless white gown at his work, who handled large quantities of such precious commodities as butter and sugar, who was deferred to, even smiled at, by every housewife in the village.

Claud Cubbage was never quite at his ease in this house, and that was precisely as Mr. Hoddy intended it. They were sitting round the fire in the parlour with cups of tea in their hands, Mr. Hoddy in the best chair to the right of the fireplace, Claud and Clarice on the sofa, decorously separated by a wide space. The younger daughter, Ada, was on a hard upright chair to the left, and they made a little circle round the fire, a stiff, tense little circle, primly tea-sipping.

"Yes, Mr. Hoddy," Claud was saying, "you can be quite sure both Gordon and me's got quite a number of nice little ideas up our sleeves this very moment. It's only a question of taking our time and making sure which is going to be the most profitable."

"What sort of ideas?" Mr. Hoddy asked, fixing Claud with his small, disapproving eyes.

"Ah, there you are now. That's it, you see." Claud shifted uncomfortably on the sofa. His blue lounge suit was tight around his chest, and it was especially tight between his legs, up in the crotch. The tightness in his crotch was actually painful to him and he wanted terribly to hitch it downward.

"This man you call Gordon, I thought he had a profitable business out there as it is," Mr. Hoddy said. "Why does he want to change?"

"Absolutely right, Mr. Hoddy. It's a first-rate business. But it's a good thing to keep expanding, see. New ideas is what we're after. Something I can come in on as well and take a share of the profits."

"Such as what?"

Mr. Hoddy was eating a slice of currant cake, nibbling it round the edges, and his small mouth was like the mouth of a caterpillar biting a tiny curved slice out of the edge of a leaf.

"Such as what?" he asked again.

"There's long conferences, Mr. Hoddy, takes place every day between Gordon and me about these different matters of business."

"Such as what?" he repeated, relentless.

Clarice glanced sideways at Claud, encouraging. Claud turned his large slow eyes upon Mr. Hoddy, and he was silent. He wished Mr. Hoddy wouldn't push him around like this, always shooting questions at him and glaring at him and acting just exactly like he was the bloody adjutant or something.

"Such as what?" Mr. Hoddy said, and this time Claud knew that he was not going to let go. Also, his instinct warned him that the old man was trying to create a crisis.

"Well now," he said, breathing deep. "I don't really want to go into details until we got it properly worked out. All we're doing so far is turning our ideas over in our minds, see."

"All I'm asking," Mr. Hoddy said irritably, "is what *sort* of business are you contemplating? I presume that it's respectable?"

"Now *please*, Mr. Hoddy. You don't for one moment think we'd even so much as *consider* anything that wasn't absolutely and entirely respectable, do you?"

Mr. Hoddy grunted, stirring his tea slowly, watching Claud. Clarice sat mute and fearful on the sofa, gazing into the fire.

"I've never been in favour of starting a business," Mr. Hoddy pronounced, defending his own failure in that line. "A good respectable job is all a man should wish for. A respectable job in respectable surroundings. Too much hokey-pokey in business for my liking."

"The thing is this," Claud said, desperate now. "All I want is to provide my wife with everything she can possibly desire. A house to live in and furniture and a flower garden and a washing machine and all the best things in the world. That's what I want to do and you can't do that on an ordinary wage now, can you? It's impossible to get enough money to do that unless you go into business, Mr. Hoddy. You'll surely agree with me there?"

Mr. Hoddy, who had worked for an ordinary wage all his life, didn't much like this point of view.

"And don't you think *I* provide everything my family wants, might I ask?"

"Oh yes and more!" Claud cried fervently. "But *you've* got a very superior job, Mr. Hoddy, and that makes all the difference."

"But what *sort* of business are you thinking of?" the man persisted.

Claud sipped his tea to give himself a little more time and he couldn't help wondering how the miserable old bastard's face would look if he simply up and told him the truth right there and then, if he'd said, "What we've got,

Mr. Hoddy, if you really want to know, is a couple of greyhounds and one's a perfect ringer for the other and we're going to bring off the biggest goddam gamble in the history of flapping, see." He'd like to watch the old bastard's face if he said that, he really would.

They were all waiting for him to proceed now, sitting there with cups of tea in their hands, staring at him and waiting for him to say something good. "Well," he said, speaking very slowly because he was thinking deep. "I've been pondering something a long time now, something as'll make more money even than Gordon's secondhand cars or anything else come to that, and practically no expense involved." That's better, he told himself. Keep going along like that.

"And what might that be?"

"Something so queer, Mr. Hoddy, there isn't one in a million would even believe it."

"Well, what is it?" Mr. Hoddy placed his cup carefully on the little table beside him and leaned forward to listen. And Claud, watching him, knew more than ever that this man and all those like him were his enemies. It was the Mr. Hoddys were the trouble. They were all the same. He knew them all, with their clean ugly hands, their grey skin, their acrid mouths, their tendency to develop little round bulging bellies just below the waistcoat; and always the unctuous curl of the nose, the weak chin, the suspicious eyes that were dark and moved too quick. The Mr. Hoddys. Oh Christ.

"Well, what is it?"

"It's an absolute gold mine, Mr. Hoddy, honestly it is."

"I'll believe that when I hear it."

"It's a thing so simple and amazing most people

wouldn't even bother to do it." He had it now—something he *had* actually been thinking seriously about for a long time, something he'd always wanted to do. He leaned across and put his teacup carefully on the table beside Mr. Hoddy's, then, not knowing what to do with his hands, placed them on his knees, palms downward.

"Well, come on, man, what is it?"

"It's maggots," Claud answered softly.

Mr. Hoddy jerked back as though someone had squirted water in his face. "Maggots!" he said, aghast. "*Maggots?* What on earth do you mean, maggots?" Claud had forgotten that this word was almost unmentionable in any self-respecting grocer's shop. Ada began to giggle, but Clarice glanced at her so malignantly the giggle died on her mouth.

"That's where the money is, starting a maggot factory."

"Are you trying to be funny?"

"Honestly, Mr. Hoddy, it may sound a bit queer, and that's simply because you never heard of it before, but it's a little gold mine."

"A *maggot factory!* Really now, Cubbage! Please be sensible!"

Clarice wished her father wouldn't call him Cubbage.

"You never heard speak of a maggot factory, Mr. Hoddy?"

"I certainly have not!"

"There's maggot factories going now, real big companies with managers and directors and all, and you know what, Mr. Hoddy? They're making millions!"

"Nonsense, man."

"And you know why they're making millions?" Claud paused, but he did not notice now that the listener's face was slowly turning yellow. "It's because of the enormous demand for maggots, Mr. Hoddy."

At that moment, Mr. Hoddy was listening also to other voices, the voices of his customers across the counter—Mrs. Rabbits's, for instance, as he sliced off her ration of butter, Mrs. Rabbits with her brown moustache and always talking so loud and saying well well well; he could hear her now saying, Well well well, Mr. Hoddy, so your Clarice got married last week, did she. Very nice too, I must say, and what was it you said her husband does, Mr. Hoddy?

He owns a maggot factory, Mrs. Rabbits.

No thank you, he told himself, watching Claud with his small, hostile eyes. No thank you very much indeed. I don't want that.

"I can't say," he announced primly, "that I myself have ever had occasion to purchase a maggot."

"Now you come to mention it, Mr. Hoddy, nor have I. Nor has many other people we know. But let me ask you something else. How many times you had occasion to purchase . . . a crown wheel and pinion, for instance?"

This was a shrewd question and Claud permitted himself a slow mawkish smile.

"What's that got to do with maggots?"

"Exactly this—that certain people buy certain things, see. You never bought a crown wheel and pinion in your life, but that don't say there isn't men getting rich this very moment making them—because there is. It's the same with maggots!"

"Would you mind telling me who these unpleasant people are who buy maggots?"

"Maggots are bought by fishermen, Mr. Hoddy. Amateur fishermen. There's thousands and thousands of fishermen all over the country going out every weekend fishing the rivers and all of them wanting maggots. Willing to pay good money for them, too. You go along the river there anywhere you like above Marlow on a Sunday and you'll see them *lining* the banks. Sitting there one beside the other, simply *lining* the banks on both sides."

"Those men don't buy maggots. They go down the bottom of the garden and dig worms."

"Now that's just where you're wrong, Mr. Hoddy, if

you'll allow me to say so. That's just where you're absolutely wrong. They want maggots, not worms."

"In that case, they get their own maggots."

"They don't *want* to get their own maggots. Just imagine, Mr. Hoddy, it's Saturday afternoon and you're going out fishing and a nice clean tin of maggots arrives by post and all you've got to do is slip it in the fishing bag and away you go. You don't think fellers is going out digging for worms and hunting for maggots when they can have them delivered right to their very doorsteps like that just for a bob or two, do you?"

"And might I ask how you propose to run this maggot factory of yours?" When he spoke the word "maggot," it

seemed as if he were spitting out a sour little pip from his mouth.

"Easiest thing in the world to run a maggot factory." Claud was gaining confidence now and warming to his subject. "All you need is a couple of old oil drums and a few lumps of rotten meat or a sheep's head, and you put them in the oil drums and that's all you do. The flies do the rest."

Had he been watching Mr. Hoddy's face, he would probably have stopped there.

"Of course, it's not quite as easy as it sounds. What you've got to do next is feed up your maggots with special diet. Bran and milk. And then when they get big and fat you put them in pint tins and post them off to your customers. Five shillings a pint they fetch. *Five shillings a pint!*" he cried, slapping his knee. "You just imagine that, Mr. Hoddy! And they say one bluebottle'll lay twenty pints easy!"

He paused again, but merely to marshal his thoughts, for there was no stopping him now.

"And there's another thing, Mr. Hoddy. A good maggot factory don't just breed ordinary maggots, you know. Every fisherman's got his own tastes. Maggots are commonest, but also there's lugworms. Some fishermen won't have nothing but lugworms. And of course there's coloured maggots. Ordinary maggots are white, but you get them all sorts of different colours by feeding them special foods, see. Red ones and green ones and black ones, and you can even get blue ones if you know what to feed them. The most difficult thing of all in a maggot factory is a blue maggot, Mr. Hoddy."

Claud stopped to catch his breath. He was having a vision now—the same vision that accompanied all his dreams of wealth—of an immense factory building with tall chimneys and hundreds of happy workers streaming in through the wide wrought-iron gates and Claud himself sitting in his luxurious office directing operations with a calm and splendid assurance.

"There's people with brains studying these things this very minute," he went on. "So you got to jump in quick unless you want to get left out in the cold. That's the secret of big business, jumping in quick before all the others, Mr. Hoddy."

Clarice, Ada, and the father sat absolutely still, looking straight ahead. None of them moved or spoke. Only Claud rushed on.

"Just so long as you make sure your maggots is alive when you post 'em. They've got to be wiggling, see. Maggots is no good unless they're wiggling. And when we really get going, when we've built up a little capital, then we'll put up some glasshouses."

Another pause, and Claud stroked his chin. "Now I expect you're all wondering why a person should want glasshouses in a maggot factory. Well—I'll tell you. It's for the flies in the winter, see. Most important to take care of your flies in the winter."

"I think that's enough, thank you, Cubbage," Mr. Hoddy said suddenly.

Claud looked up and for the first time he saw the expression on the man's face. It stopped him cold.

"I don't want to hear any more about it," Mr. Hoddy said.

"All I'm trying to do, Mr. Hoddy," Claud cried, "is give your little girl everything she can possibly desire. That's all I'm thinking of night and day, Mr. Hoddy."

"Then all I hope is you'll be able to do it without the help of maggots."

"Dad!" Clarice cried, alarmed. "I simply won't have you talking to Claud like that."

"I'll talk to him how I wish, thank you, miss."

"I think it's time I was getting along," Claud said. "Good night."

Mr. Feasey

WE WERE both up early when the big day came.

I wandered into the kitchen for a shave, but Claud got dressed right away and went outside to arrange about the straw. The kitchen was a front room, and through the window I could see the sun just coming up behind the line of trees on top of the ridge the other side of the valley.

Each time Claud came past the window with an armload of straw, I noticed over the rim of the mirror the intent, breathless expression on his face, the great round bullethead thrusting forward and the forehead wrinkled into deep corrugations right up to the hairline. I'd only seen this look on him once before, and that was the evening he'd asked Clarice to marry him. Today he was so excited he even walked funny, treading softly as though the concrete around the filling station were a shade too hot for the soles of his feet; and he kept packing more and more straw into the back of the van to make it comfortable for Jackie.

Then he came into the kitchen to fix breakfast, and I watched him put the pot of soup on the stove and begin stirring it. He had a long metal spoon and he kept on

stirring and stirring all the time it was coming to the boil, and about every half minute he leaned forward and stuck his nose into that sickly-sweet steam of cooking horseflesh. Then he started putting extras into it—three peeled onions, a few young carrots, a cupful of stinging-nettle tops, a teaspoon of Valentine's Meatjuice, twelve drops of cod-liver oil—and everything he touched was handled very gently with the ends of his big fat fingers as though it might have been a little fragment of Venetian glass. He took some minced horsemeat from the icebox, measured one handful into Jackie's bowl, three into the other, and when the soup was ready he shared it out between the two, pouring it over the meat.

It was the same ceremony I'd seen performed each morning for the past five months, but never with such intense and breathless concentration as this. There was no talk, not even a glance my way, and when he turned and went out again to fetch the dogs, even the back of his neck and the shoulders seemed to be whispering, "Oh Jesus, don't let anything go wrong, and especially don't let me *do* anything wrong today."

I heard him talking softly to the dogs in the pen as he put the leashes on them, and when he brought them around into the kitchen, they came in prancing and pulling to get at the breakfast, treading up and down with their front feet and waving their enormous tails from side to side, like whips.

"All right," Claud said, speaking at last. "Which is it?"

Most mornings he'd offer to bet me a pack of cigarettes, but there were bigger things at stake today and I knew all he wanted for the moment was a little extra reassurance.

He watched me as I walked once around the two beautiful, identical, tall velvety-black dogs, and he moved aside, holding the leashes at arms' length to give me a better view.

"Jackie!" I said, trying the old trick that never worked. "Hey, Jackie!" Two identical heads with identical expressions flicked around to look at me, four bright, identical deep-yellow eyes stared into mine. There'd been a time when I fancied the eyes of one were a slightly darker yellow than those of the other. There'd also been a time when I thought I could recognise Jackie because of a deeper brisket and a shade more muscle on the hindquarters. But it wasn't so.

"Come on," Claud said. He was hoping that today of all days I would make a bad guess.

"This one," I said. "This is Jackie."

"Which?"

"This one on the left."

"There!" he cried, his whole face suddenly beaming. "You're wrong again!"

"I don't think I'm wrong."

"You're about as wrong as you could possibly be. And now listen, Gordon, and I'll tell you something. All these last weeks, every morning while you've been trying to pick him out—you know what?"

"What?"

"I've been keeping count. And the result is you haven't been right even *one-half* the time! You'd have done better tossing a coin!"

What he meant was that if I (who saw them every day and side by side) couldn't do it, why the hell should we be frightened of Mr. Feasey. Claud knew Mr. Feasey was famous for spotting ringers, but he knew also that it could be very difficult to tell the difference between two dogs when there wasn't any.

He put the bowls of food on the floor, giving Jackie the one with the least meat because he was running today. When he stood back to watch them eat, the shadow of deep concern was back again on his face and the large pale eyes were staring at Jackie with the same rapt and melting look of love that up till recently had been reserved only for Clarice.

"You see, Gordon," he said. "It's just what I've always told you. For the last hundred years there's been all manner of ringers, some good and some bad, but in the whole history of dog racing there's never been a ringer like this."

"I hope you're right," I said, and my mind began travelling back to that freezing afternoon just before Christmas, four months ago, when Claud had asked to borrow the van and had driven away in the direction of Aylesbury without saying where he was going. I had assumed he was off to see Clarice, but late in the afternoon he had returned bringing with him this dog he said he'd bought off a man for thirty-five shillings.

"Is he fast?" I had said. We were standing out by the pumps and Claud was holding the dog on a leash and looking at him, and a few snowflakes were falling and settling on the dog's back. The motor of the van was still running.

"Fast!" Claud had said. "He's just about the slowest dog you ever saw in your whole life!"

"Then what you buy him for?"

"Well," he had said, the big bovine face secret and cunning, "it occurred to me that maybe he might possibly look a little bit like Jackie. What d'you think?"

"I suppose he does a bit, now you come to mention it."

He had handed me the leash and I had taken the new dog inside to dry him off while Claud had gone round to the pen to fetch his beloved. And when he returned and we put the two of them together for the first time, I can remember him stepping back and saying, "Oh Jesus!" and standing dead still in front of them like he was seeing a phantom. Then he became very quick and quiet. He got down on his knees and began comparing them carefully point by point, and it was almost like the room was getting warmer and warmer the way I could feel his excitement growing every second through this long silent examination in which even the toenails and the dew-claws, eighteen on each dog, were matched alongside one another for colour.

"Look," he said at last, standing up. "Walk them up and down the room a few times, will you?" And then he had stayed there for quite five or six minutes leaning against the stove with his eyes half closed and his head on one side, watching them and frowning and chewing his lips. After that, as though he didn't believe what he had seen the first time, he had gone down again on his knees to recheck everything once more; but suddenly, in the middle of it, he had jumped up and looked at me, his face fixed and tense, with a curious whiteness around the nostrils and the eyes. "All right," he had said, a little tremor in his voice. "You know what? We're home. We're rich."

And then the secret conferences between us in the kitchen, the detailed planning, the selection of the most suitable track, and finally every other Saturday, eight times in all, locking up my filling station (losing a whole afternoon's custom) and driving the ringer all the way up to Oxford to a scruffy little track out in the fields near Headingley where the big money was played but which was actually nothing except a line of old posts and cord to mark the course, an upturned bicycle for pulling the dummy hare, and at the far end, in the distance, six traps and the starter. We had driven this ringer up there eight times over a period of sixteen weeks and entered him with Mr. Feasey and stood around on the edge of the crowd in freezing raining cold, waiting for his name to go up on the blackboard in chalk. The Black Panther we called him. And when his time came, Claud would always lead him down to the traps and I would stand at the finish to catch him and keep him clear of the fighters, the gypsy dogs that the gypsies so often slipped in specially to tear another one to pieces at the end of a race.

But you know, there was something rather sad about taking this dog all the way up there so many times and letting him run and watching him and hoping and praying that whatever happened he would always come last. Of course the praying wasn't necessary and we never really had a moment's worry, because the old fellow simply couldn't gallop and that's all there was to it. He ran exactly like a crab. The only time he didn't come last was when a big fawn dog by the name of Amber Flash put his foot in a hole and broke a hock and finished on three legs. But even then ours only just beat him. So this way we got him right down to bottom grade with the scrubbers, and the last time we were there all the bookies were laying him twenty or thirty to one and calling his name and begging people to back him.

Now at last, on this sunny April day, it was Jackie's turn to go instead. Claud said we mustn't run the ringer anymore or Mr. Feasey might begin to get tired of him and throw him out altogether, he was so slow. Claud said this was the exact psychological time to have it off, and that Jackie would win it anything between thirty and fifty lengths.

He had raised Jackie from a pup and the dog was only fifteen months now, but he was a good fast runner. He'd never raced yet, but we knew he was fast from clocking him round the little private schooling track at Uxbridge where Claud had taken him every Sunday since he was seven months old—except once when he was having some inoculations. Claud said he probably wasn't fast enough to win top grade at Mr. Feasey's, but where we'd got him now, in bottom grade with the scrubbers, he could fall over and get up again and still win it twenty—well, anyway ten or fifteen lengths, Claud said.

So all I had to do this morning was go to the bank in the village and draw out fifty pounds for myself and fifty for Claud, which I would lend him as an advance against wages, and then at twelve o'clock lock up the filling station and hang the notice on one of the pumps saying "GONE FOR THE DAY." Claud would shut the ringer in the

pen at the back and put Jackie in the van and off we'd go. I won't say I was as excited as Claud, but there again I didn't have all sorts of important things depending on it, either, like buying a house and being able to get married. Nor was I almost *born* in a kennel with greyhounds, as he was, walking about thinking of absolutely nothing else all day—except perhaps Clarice in the evenings. Personally, I had my own career as a filling-station owner to keep me busy, not to mention secondhand cars, but if Claud wanted to fool around with dogs, that was all right with me, especially a thing like today—if it came off. As a matter of fact, I don't mind admitting that every time I thought about the money we were putting on and the money we might win, my stomach gave a little lurch.

The dogs had finished their breakfast now, and Claud took them out for a short walk across the field opposite while I got dressed and fried the eggs. Afterwards, I went to the bank and drew out the money (all in ones), and the rest of the morning seemed to go very quickly serving customers.

At twelve sharp I locked up and hung the notice on the pump. Claud came around from the back leading Jackie and carrying a large suitcase made of reddish-brown cardboard.

"Suitcase?"

"For the money," Claud answered. "You said yourself no man can carry two thousand pound in his pockets."

It was a lovely yellow spring day with the buds bursting all along the hedges and the sun shining through the new pale-green leaves on the big beech tree across the road. Jackie looked wonderful, with two big hard muscles the size of melons bulging on his hindquarters, his coat glistening like black velvet. While Claud was putting the suitcase in the van, the dog did a little prancing jib on his toes to show how fit he was; then he looked up at me and grinned, just like he knew he was off to the races to win two thousand pounds and a heap of glory. This Jackie had the widest, most human-smiling grin I ever saw. Not only did he lift his upper lip, but he actually stretched the corners of his mouth so you could see every tooth in his head except perhaps one or two of the molars right at the back, and every time I saw him do it I found myself waiting to hear him start laughing out loud as well.

We got in the van and off we went. I was doing the driving. Claud was beside me and Jackie was standing up on the straw in the rear looking over our shoulders through the windshield. Claud kept turning round and trying to make him lie down, so he wouldn't get thrown whenever we went round the sharp corners, but the dog was too excited to do anything except grin back at him, and wave his enormous tail.

"You got the money, Gordon?" Claud was chain-smoking cigarettes and quite unable to sit still.

"Yes."

"Mine as well?"

"I got a hundred and five altogether. Five for the winder like you said, so he won't stop the hare and make it a no-race."

"Good," Claud said, rubbing his hands together hard as though he were freezing cold. "Good good good."

We drove through the little narrow High Street of Great Missenden and caught a glimpse of old Rummins going into The Nag's Head for his morning pint; then outside the village we turned left and climbed over the ridge of the Chilterns towards Princes Risborough, and from there it would only be twenty-odd miles to Oxford.

And now a silence and a kind of tension began to come over us both. We sat very quiet, not speaking at all, each nursing his own fears and excitements, containing his anxiety. And Claud kept smoking his cigarettes and throwing them half finished out the window. Usually, on these trips, he talked his head off all the way there and back, all the things he'd done with dogs in his life, the jobs he'd pulled, the places he'd been, the money he'd won; and all the things other people had done with dogs, the thievery, the cruelty, the unbelievable trickery and cunning of owners at the flapping tracks. But today I don't think he was trusting himself to speak very much. At this point, for that matter, nor was I. I was sitting there watching the road and trying to keep my mind off the immediate future by thinking back on all that stuff Claud had told me about this curious greyhound-racing racket.

I swear there wasn't a man alive who knew more about it than Claud did, and ever since we'd got the ringer and decided to pull this job, he'd taken it upon himself to give me an education in the business. By now—in theory, at any rate—I suppose I knew nearly as much as him.

It had started during the very first strategy conference we'd had in the kitchen. I can remember it was the day after the ringer arrived and we were sitting there watching for customers through the window, and Claud was explaining to me all about what we'd have to do, and I was trying to follow him as best I could until finally there came one question I had to ask.

"What I don't see," I had said, "is why you use the ringer at all. Wouldn't it be safer if we use Jackie all the time and simply stop him the first half-dozen races so he comes last? Then when we're good and ready, we can let him go. Same result in the end, wouldn't it be, if we do it right? And no danger of being caught."

Well, as I say, that did it. Claud looked up at me quickly and said, "Hey! None of that! I'd just like you to know 'stopping's' something I never do. What's come over you, Gordon?" He seemed genuinely pained and shocked by what I had said.

"I don't see anything wrong with it."

"Now listen to me, Gordon. Stopping a good dog breaks his heart. A good dog knows he's fast, and seeing all the others out there in front and not being able to catch them—it breaks his heart, I tell you. And what's more, you wouldn't be making suggestions like that if you knew some of the tricks them fellers do to stop their dogs at the flapping tracks."

"Such as what, for example?" I had asked.

"Such as anything in the world almost, so long as it makes the dog go slower. And it takes a lot of stopping, a good greyhound does. Full of guts and so mad keen you can't even let them watch a race—they'll tear the leash right out of your hand rearing to go. Many's the time I've seen one with a broken leg insisting on finishing the race."

He had paused then, looking at me thoughtfully with those large pale eyes, serious as hell and obviously thinking deep. "Maybe," he had said, "if we're going to do this job properly, I'd better tell you a thing or two so's you'll know what we're up against."

"Go ahead and tell me," I had said. "I'd like to know."

For a moment he stared in silence out the window. "The main thing you got to remember," he had said darkly, "is that all these fellers going to the flapping tracks with dogs—they're artful. They're more artful than you could possibly imagine." Again he paused, marshalling his thoughts.

"Now take for example the different ways of stopping a dog. The first, the commonest, is strapping."

"Strapping?"

"Yes. Strapping 'em up. That's commonest. Pulling the muzzle strap tight around their necks so they can't hardly breathe, see. A clever man knows just which hole on the strap to use and just how many lengths it'll take off his dog in a race. Usually a couple of notches is good for five or six lengths. Do it up real tight and he'll come last.

I've known plenty of dogs collapse and die from being strapped up tight on a hot day. Strangulated, absolutely strangulated, and a very nasty thing it was too. Then again, some of 'em just tie two of the toes together with black cotton. Dog never runs well like that. Unbalances him."

"That doesn't sound too bad."

"Then there's others that put a piece of fresh-chewed gum up under their tails, right up close where the tail joins the body. And there's nothing funny about that," he had said, indignant. "The tail of a running dog goes up and down ever so slightly and the gum on the tail keeps sticking to the hairs on the backside, just where it's tenderest. No dogs likes that, you know. Then there's sleeping pills. That's used a lot nowadays. They do it by weight, exactly like a doctor, and they measure the powder according to whether they want to slow him up five or ten or fifteen lengths. Those are just a few of the ordinary ways," he had said. "Actually they're nothing. Absolutely nothing compared with some of the other things that's done to hold a dog back in a race, especially by the gypsies. There's things the gypsies do that are almost too disgusting to mention, such as when they're just putting the dog in the trap, things you wouldn't hardly do to your worst enemies."

And when he had told me about those—which were, indeed, terrible things because they had to do with physical injury, quickly, painfully inflicted—then he had gone on to tell me what they did when they wanted the dog to win.

"There's just as terrible things done to make 'em go fast as to make 'em go slow," he had said softly, his face veiled and secret. "And perhaps the commonest of all is wintergreen. Whenever you see a dog going around with no hair on his back or little bald patches all over him—that's wintergreen. Just before the race they rub it hard into the skin. Sometimes it's Sloan's Liniment, but mostly it's wintergreen. Stings terrible. Stings so bad that all the old dog wants to do is run run run as fast as he possibly can to get away from the pain.

"Then there's special drugs they give with the needle. Mind you, that's the modern method and most of the spivs at the track are too ignorant to use it. It's the fellers coming down from London in the big cars with stadium dogs they've borrowed for the day by bribing the trainer—they're the ones use the needle."

I could remember him sitting there at the kitchen table with a cigarette dangling from his mouth and dropping his eyelids to keep out the smoke and looking at me through his wrinkled, nearly closed eyes, and saying, "What you've got to remember, Gordon, is this. There's nothing they won't do to make a dog win if they want him to. On the other hand, no dog can run faster than he's built, no matter what they do to him. So if we can get Jackie down into bottom grade, then we're home. No dog in bottom grade can get near him, not even with wintergreen and needles. Not even with ginger."

"Ginger?"

"Certainly. That's a common one, ginger is. What they do, they take a piece of raw ginger about the size of a walnut, and about five minutes before the off they slip it into the dog."

"You mean in his mouth? He eats it?"

"No," he had said. "Not in his mouth."

And so it had gone on. During each of the eight long trips we had subsequently made to the track with the ringer, I had heard more and more about this charming sport—more, especially, about the methods of stopping them and making them go (even the names of the drugs and the quantities to use). I heard about "the rat treatment" (for non-chasers, to make them chase the dummy hare), where a rat is placed in a can which is then tied around the dog's neck. There's a small hole in the lid of the can just large enough for the rat to poke its head out and nip the dog. But the dog can't get at the rat, and so naturally he goes half crazy running around and being bitten in the neck, and the more he shakes the can the more the rat bites him. Finally, someone releases the rat, and the dog, who up to then was a nice docile tail-wagging animal who wouldn't hurt a mouse, pounces on it in a rage and tears it to pieces. Do this a few times, Claud had said—"mind you, I don't hold with it myself"—and the dog becomes a real killer who will chase anything, even the dummy hare.

We were over the Chilterns now and running down out of the beechwoods into the flat elm- and oak-tree country south of Oxford. Claud sat quietly beside me, nursing his nervousness and smoking cigarettes, and every two or three minutes he would turn round to see if Jackie was all right. The dog was at last lying down, and each time Claud turned round, he whispered something to him softly, and the dog acknowledged his words with a faint movement of the tail that made the straw rustle.

Soon we would be coming into Thame, the broad High Street where they penned the pigs and cows and sheep on market day, and where the Fair came once a year with the swings and roundabouts and bumping cars and gypsy caravans right there in the street in the middle of the town. Claud was born in Thame, and we'd never driven through it yet without him mentioning this fact.

"Well," he said as the first houses came into sight, "here's Thame. I was born and bred in Thame, you know, Gordon."

"You told me."

"Lots of funny things we used to do around here when we was nippers," he said, slightly nostalgic.

"I'm sure."

He paused, and I think more to relieve the tension building up inside him than anything else, he began talking about the years of his youth.

"There was a boy next door," he said. "Gilbert Gomm his name was. Little sharp ferrety face and one leg a bit shorter'n the other. Shocking things him and me used to do together. You know one thing we done, Gordon?"

"What?"

"We'd go into the kitchen Saturday nights when Mum and Dad were at the pub, and we'd disconnect the pipe from the gas ring and bubble the gas into a milk bottle full of water. Then we'd sit down and drink it out of teacups."

"Was that so good?"

"Good! It was absolutely disgusting! But we'd put lashings of sugar in and then it didn't taste so bad."

"Why did you drink it?"

Claud turned and looked at me, incredulous. "You mean you never drunk 'snake's water'!"

"Can't say I have."

"I thought everyone done that when they was kids! It

intoxicates you, just like wine only worse, depending on how long you let the gas bubble through. We used to get reeling drunk together there in the kitchen Saturday nights and it was marvellous. Until one night Dad comes home early and catches us. I'll never forget that night as long as I live. There was me holding the milk bottle, and the gas bubbling through it lovely, and Gilbert kneeling on the floor ready to turn off the tap the moment I give the word, and in walks Dad."

"What did he say?"

"Oh Christ, Gordon, that was terrible. He didn't say one word, but he stands there by the door and he starts feeling for his belt, undoing the buckle very slow and pulling the belt slow out of his trousers, looking at me all the time. Great big feller he was, with great big hands like coalhammers and a black moustache and them little purple veins running all over his cheeks. Then he comes over quick and grabs me by the coat and lets me have it, hard as he can, using the end with the buckle on it, and honest to God, Gordon, I thought he was going to kill me. But in the end he stops and then he puts on the belt again, slow and careful, buckling it up and tucking in the flap and belching with the beer he'd drunk. And then he walks out again back to the pub, still without saying a word. Worst hiding I ever had in my life."

"How old were you then?"

"Round about eight, I should think," Claud said.

As we drew closer to Oxford, he became silent again. He kept twisting his neck to see if Jackie was all right, to touch him, to stroke his head, and once he turned around and knelt on the seat to gather more straw around the dog, murmuring something about a draught. We drove around the fringe of Oxford and into a network of narrow country roads, and after a while we turned into a small bumpy lane and along this we began to overtake a thin stream of men and women all walking and cycling in the same direction. Some of the men were leading greyhounds. There was a large saloon car in front of us and through the rear window we could see a dog sitting on the back seat between two men.

"They come from all over," Claud said darkly. "That one there's probably come up special from London. Probably slipped him out from one of the big stadium kennels just for the afternoon. That could be a Derby dog probably, for all we know."

"Hope he's not running against Jackie."

"Don't worry," Claud said. "All new dogs automatically go in top grade. That's one rule Mr. Feasey's very particular about."

There was an open gate leading into a field, and Mr. Feasey's wife came forward to take our admission money before we drove in.

"He'd have her winding the bloody pedals too if she had the strength," Claud said. "Old Feasey don't employ more people than he has to."

I drove across the field and parked at the end of a line of cars along the top hedge. We both got out and Claud went quickly round the back to fetch Jackie. I stood beside the car, waiting. It was a very large field with a steepish slope on it, and we were at the top of the slope, looking down. In the distance I could see the six starting traps and the wooden posts marking the track, which ran along the bottom of the field and turned sharp at right angles and came on up the hill towards the crowd, to the finish.

Thirty yards beyond the finishing line stood the up-turned bicycle for driving the hare. Because it is portable, this is the standard machine for hare driving used at all flapping tracks. It comprises a flimsy wooden platform about eight feet high, supported on four poles knocked into the ground. On top of the platform there is fixed, upside down with wheels in the air, an ordinary old bicycle. The rear wheel is to the front, facing down the track, and from it the tire has been removed, leaving a concave metal rim. One end of the cord that pulls the hare is attached to this rim, and the winder (or hare driver), by straddling the bicycle at the back and turning the pedals with his hands, revolves the wheel and winds in the cord around the rim. This pulls the dummy hare toward him at any speed he likes up to forty miles an hour. After each race someone takes the dummy hare (with cord attached) all the way down to the starting traps again, thus unwinding the cord on the wheel, ready for a fresh start. From his high platform, the winder can watch the race and regulate the speed of the hare to keep it just ahead of the leading dog. He can also stop the hare any time he wants and make it a no-race (if the wrong dog looks like winning) by suddenly turning the pedals backwards and getting the cord tangled up in the hub of the wheel. The other way of doing it is to slow down the hare suddenly, for perhaps one second, and that makes the lead dog automatically check a little so that the others catch up with him. He is an important man, the winder.

I could see Mr. Feasey's winder already standing atop his platform, a powerful-looking man in a blue sweater, leaning on the bicycle and looking down at the crowd through the smoke of his cigarette.

There is a curious law in England which permits race meetings of this kind to be held only seven times a year over one piece of ground. That is why all Mr. Feasey's equipment was movable, and after the seventh meeting he would simply transfer to the next field. The law didn't bother him at all.

There was already a good crowd and the bookmakers were erecting their stands in a line over to the right. Claud had Jackie out of the van now and was leading him over to a group of people clustered around a small stocky man dressed in riding breeches—Mr. Feasey himself. Each person in the group had a dog on a leash, and Mr. Feasey kept writing names in a notebook that he held folded in his left hand. I sauntered over to watch.

"Which you got there?" Mr. Feasey said, pencil poised above the notebook.

"Midnight," a man said who was holding a black dog.

Mr. Feasey stepped back a pace and looked most carefully at the dog.

"Midnight. Right. I got him down."

"Jane," the next man said.

"Let me look. Jane . . . Jane . . . yes, all right."

"Soldier." This dog was led by a tall man with long teeth who wore a dark-blue, double-breasted lounge suit, shiny with wear, and when he said "Soldier" he began slowly to scratch the seat of his trousers with the hand that wasn't holding the leash.

Mr. Feasey bent down to examine the dog. The other man looked up at the sky.

"Take him away," Mr. Feasey said.

The man looked down quick and stopped scratching.

"Go on, take him away."

"Listen, Mr. Feasey," the man said, lisping slightly through his long teeth. "Now don't talk so bloody silly, *please.*"

"Go on and beat it, Larry, and stop wasting my time. You know as well as I do the Soldier's got two white toes on his off fore."

"Now look, Mr. Feasey," the man said. "You ain't even seen Soldier for six months at least."

"Come on now, Larry, and beat it. I haven't got time arguing with you." Mr. Feasey didn't appear the least angry. "Next," he said.

I saw Claud step forward leading Jackie. The large bovine face was fixed and wooden, the eyes staring at something about a yard above Mr. Feasey's head, and he was holding the leash so tight his knuckles were like a row of little white onions. I knew just how he was feeling.

I felt the same way myself at that moment, and it was even worse when Mr. Feasey suddenly started laughing.

"Hey!" he cried. "Here's the Black Panther. Here's the champion."

"That's right, Mr. Feasey," Claud said.

"Well, I'll tell you," Mr. Feasey said, still grinning. "You can take him right back home where he come from. I don't want him."

"But look here, Mr. Feasey—"

"Six or eight times at least, I've run him for you now and that's enough. Look—why don't you shoot him and have done with it?"

"Now listen, Mr. Feasey, *please*. Just once more and I'll never ask you again."

"Not even once! I got more dogs than I can handle here today. There's no room for crabs like that."

I thought Claud was going to cry.

"Now honest, Mr. Feasey," he said. "I been up at six every morning this past two weeks giving him roadwork and massage and buying him beefsteaks, and believe me he's a different dog absolutely than what he was last time he run."

The words "different dog" caused Mr. Feasey to jump as if he'd been pricked with a hatpin. "What's that!" he cried. "Different dog!"

I'll say this for Claud, he kept his head. "See here, Mr. Feasey," he said. "I'll thank you not to go implying things to me. You know very well I didn't mean that."

"All right, all right. But just the same, you can take him away. There's no sense running dogs as slow as him. Take him home now, will you please, and don't hold up the whole meeting."

I was watching Claud. Claud was watching Mr. Feasey. Mr. Feasey was looking round for the next dog to enter up. Under his brown tweedy jacket he wore a yellow pullover, and this streak of yellow on his breast and his thin gaitered legs and the way he jerked his head from side to side made him seem like some sort of a little perky bird—a goldfinch, perhaps.

Claud took a step forward. His face was beginning to purple slightly with the outrage of it all and I could see his Adam's apple moving up and down as he swallowed.

"I'll tell you what I'll do, Mr. Feasey. I'm so absolutely sure this dog's improved I'll bet you a quid he don't finish last. There you are."

Mr. Feasey turned slowly around and looked at Claud. "You crackers?" he asked.

"I'll bet you a quid, there you are, just to prove what I'm saying."

It was a dangerous move, certain to cause suspicion, but Claud knew it was the only thing left to do. There was silence while Mr. Feasey bent down and examined the dog. I could see the way his eyes were moving slowly over the animal's whole body, part by part. There was something to admire in the man's thoroughness, and in his memory; something to fear also in this self-confident little rogue who held in his head the shape and colour and markings of perhaps several hundred different but very similar dogs. He never needed more than one little clue—a small scar, a splay toe, a trifle in at the hocks, a less pronounced wheelback, a slightly darker brindle—Mr. Feasey always remembered.

So I watched him now as he bent down over Jackie. His face was pink and fleshy, the mouth small and tight as though it couldn't stretch enough to make a smile, and the eyes were like two little cameras focused sharply on the dog.

"Well," he said, straightening up. "It's the same dog, anyway."

"I should hope so too!" Claud cried. "Just what sort of a fellow you think I am, Mr. Feasey?"

"I think you're crackers, that's what I think. But it's a nice easy way to make a quid. I suppose you forgot how Amber Flash nearly beat him on three legs last meeting?"

"This one wasn't fit then," Claud said. "He hadn't had beefsteak and massage and roadwork like I've been giving him lately. But look, Mr. Feasey, you're not to go sticking him in top grade just to win the bet. This is a bottom-grade dog, Mr. Feasey. You know that."

Mr. Feasey laughed. The small button mouth opened into a tiny circle and he laughed and looked at the crowd, who laughed with him. "Listen," he said, laying a hairy hand on Claud's shoulder. "I know my dogs. I don't have to do any fiddling around to win *this* quid. He goes in bottom."

"Right," Claud said. "That's a bet." He walked away with Jackie and I joined him.

"Jesus, Gordon, that was a near one!"

"Shook me."

"But we're in now," Claud said. He had that breathless look on his face again and he was walking about quick and funny, like the ground was burning his feet.

People were still coming through the gate into the field and there were easily three hundred of them now. Not a very nice crowd. Sharp-nosed men and women with dirty faces and bad teeth and quick shifty eyes. The dregs of the big town. Oozing out like sewage from a cracked pipe and trickling along the road through the gate and making a smelly little pond of sewage at the top end of the field. They were all there, all the spivs and the gypsies and the touts and the dregs and the sewage and the scrapings and the scum from the cracked drainpipes of the big town. Some with dogs, some without. Dogs led about on pieces of string, miserable dogs with hanging heads, thin mangy dogs with sores on their quarters (from sleeping on board), sad old dogs with grey muzzles, doped dogs, dogs stuffed with porridge to stop them winning, dogs walking stiff-legged—one especially, a white one. "Claud, why is that white one walking so stiff-legged?"

"Which one?"

"That one over there."

"Ah yes, I see. Very probably because he's been hung."

"Hung?"

"Yes, hung. Suspended in a harness for twenty-four hours with his legs dangling."

"Good God, but why?"

"To make him run slow, of course. Some people don't hold with dope or stuffing or strapping up. So they hang 'em."

"I see."

"Either that," Claud said, "or they sandpaper them. Rub their pads with rough sandpaper and take the skin off so it hurts when they run."

"Yes, I see."

And then the fitter, brighter-looking dogs, the better-fed ones who get horsemeat every day, not pig swill or rusk and cabbage water, their coats shinier, their tails moving, pulling at their leads, undoped, unstuffed, awaiting perhaps a more unpleasant fate, the muzzle strap to be tightened an extra four notches. *But make sure he can breathe now, Jock. Don't choke him completely. Don't let's have him collapse in the middle of the race. Just so he wheezes a bit, see. Go on tightening it up an extra notch at a time until you can hear him wheezing. You'll see his mouth open and he'll start breathing heavy. Then it's just right, but not if his eyeballs is bulging. Watch out for that, will you? Okay?*

Okay.

"Let's get away from the crowd, Gordon. It don't do Jackie no good getting excited by all these other dogs."

We walked up the slope to where the cars were parked, then back and forth in front of the line of cars, keeping the dog on the move. Inside some of the cars I could see men sitting with their dogs, and the men scowled at us through the windows as we went by.

"Watch out now, Gordon. We don't want any trouble."

"No, all right."

These were the best dogs of all, the secret ones kept in the cars and taken out quick just to be entered up (under some invented name) and put back again quick and held there till the last minute, then straight down to the traps and back again into the cars after the race so no nosy bastard gets too close a look. The trainer at the big stadium said so. *All right, he said. You can have him, but for Christsake don't let anybody recognise him. There's thousands of people know this dog, so you've got to be careful, see. And it'll cost you fifty pound.*

Very fast dogs these, but it doesn't much matter how fast they are, they probably get the needle anyway, just to make sure. One and a half c.c.s of ether, subcutaneous, done in the car, injected very slow. That'll put ten lengths on any dog. Or sometimes it's caffeine, caffeine in oil, or camphor. That makes them go too. The men in the big cars know all about that. And some of them know about whisky. But that's intravenous. Not so easy when it's intravenous. Might miss the vein. All you got to do is miss the vein and it don't work and where are you then? So it's ether, or it's caffeine, or it's camphor. *Don't give her too much of that stuff now, Jock. What does she weigh? Fifty-eight pounds. All right then, you know what the man told us. Wait a minute now. I got it written down on a piece of paper. Here it is. Point one of a c.c. per ten pounds body weight equals five lengths over three hundred yards. Wait a minute now while I work it out. Oh Christ, you better guess it. Just guess it, Jock. It'll be all right you'll find. Shouldn't be any trouble anyway, because I picked the others in the race myself. Cost me a tenner to old Feasey. A bloody tenner I give him, and dear Mr. Feasey, I says, that's for your birthday and because I love you.*

Thank you ever so much, Mr. Feasey says. Thank you, my good and trusted friend.

And for stopping them, for the men in the big cars, it's chlorbutol. That's a beauty, chlorbutol, because you can give it the night before, especially to someone else's dog. Or pethidine. Pethidine and hyoscine mixed, whatever that may be.

"Lot of fine old English sporting gentry here," Claud said.

"Certainly are."

"Watch your pockets, Gordon. You got that money hidden away?"

We walked around the back of the line of cars—between the cars and the hedge—and I saw Jackie stiffen and begin to pull forward on the leash, advancing with a stiff crouching tread. About thirty yards away there were two men. One was holding a large fawn greyhound, the dog stiff and tense like Jackie. The other was holding a sack in his hands.

"Watch," Claud whispered, "they're giving him a kill."

Out of the sack onto the grass tumbled a small white rabbit, fluffy white, young, tame. It righted itself and sat still, crouching in the hunched-up way rabbits crouch, its nose close to the ground. A frightened rabbit. Out of the sack so suddenly onto the grass with such a bump. Into the bright light. The dog was going mad with excitement now, jumping up against the leash, pawing the ground, throwing himself forward, whining. The rabbit saw the dog. It drew in its head and stayed still, paralysed with fear. The man transferred his hold to the dog's collar, and the dog twisted and jumped and tried to get free. The other man pushed the rabbit with his foot but it was too terrified to move. He pushed it again, flicking it forward with his toe like a football, and the rabbit rolled over several times, righted itself, and began to hop over the grass away from the dog. The other man released the dog, which pounced with one huge pounce upon the rabbit, and then came the squeals, not very loud but shrill and anguished and lasting rather a long time.

"There you are," Claud said. "That's a kill."

"Not sure I liked it very much."

"I told you before, Gordon. Most of 'em does it. Keens the dog up before a race."

"I still don't like it."

"Nor me. But they all do it. Even in the big stadiums the trainers do it. Proper barbary I call it."

We strolled away, and below us on the slope of the hill the crowd was thickening and the bookies' stands with the names written on them in red and gold and blue were all erected now in a long line back of the crowd, each bookie already stationed on an upturned box beside his stand, a pack of numbered cards in one hand, a piece of chalk in the other, his clerk behind him with book and pencil. Then we saw Mr. Feasey walking over to a blackboard that was nailed to a post stuck in the ground.

"He's chalking up the first race," Claud said. "Come on, quick!"

We walked rapidly down the hill and joined the crowd. Mr. Feasey was writing the runners on the blackboard,

copying names from his soft-covered notebook, and a little hush of suspense fell upon the crowd as they watched.

1. SALLY
2. THREE QUID
3. SNAILBOX LADY
4. BLACK PANTHER
5. WHISKY
6. ROCKIT

"He's in it!" Claud whispered. "First race! Trap four! Now listen, Gordon! Give me a fiver quick to show the winder."

Claud could hardly speak from excitement. That patch of whiteness had returned around his nose and eyes, and when I handed him a five-pound note, his whole arm was shaking as he took it. The man who was going to wind the bicycle pedals was still standing on top of the wooden platform in his blue jersey, smoking. Claud went over and stood below him, looking up.

"See this fiver," he said, talking softly, holding it folded small in the palm of his hand.

The man glanced at it without moving his head.

"Just so long as you wind her true this race, see. No stopping and no slowing down and run her fast. Right?"

The man didn't move but there was a slight, almost imperceptible lifting of the eyebrows. Claud turned away.

"Now look, Gordon. Get the money on gradual, all in little bits like I told you. Just keep going down the line putting on little bits so you don't kill the price, see. And I'll be walking Jackie down very slow, as slow as I dare, to give you plenty of time. Right?"

"Right."

"And don't forget to be standing ready to catch him at the end of the race. Get him clear away from all them others when they start fighting for the hare. Grab a hold of him tight and don't let go till I come running up with the collar and lead. That Whisky's a gypsy dog and he'll tear the leg off anything as gets in his way."

"Right," I said. "Here we go."

I saw Claud lead Jackie over to the finishing post and collect a yellow jacket with "4" written on it large. Also a muzzle. The other five runners were there too, the owners fussing around them, putting on their numbered jackets, adjusting their muzzles. Mr. Feasey was officiating, hopping about in his tight riding breeches like an anxious perky bird, and once I saw him say something to Claud and laugh. Claud ignored him. Soon they would all start to lead the dogs down the track, the long walk down the hill and across to the far corner of the field to the starting traps. It would take them ten minutes to walk it. I've got at least ten minutes, I told myself, and then I began to push my way through the crowd standing six or seven deep in front of the line of bookies.

"Even money Whisky! Even money Whisky! Five to two Sally! Even money Whisky! Four to one Snailbox! Come on now! Hurry up, hurry up! Which is it?"

On every board all down the line the Black Panther was chalked up at twenty-five to one. I edged forward to the nearest book.

"Three pounds Black Panther," I said, holding out the money.

The man on the box had an inflamed magenta face and traces of some white substance around the corners of his mouth. He snatched the money and dropped it in his satchel. "Seventy-five pounds to three Black Panther," he said. "Number forty-two." He handed me a ticket and his clerk recorded the bet.

I stepped back and wrote rapidly on the back of the ticket "75 to 3," then slipped it into the inside pocket of my jacket, with the money.

So long as I continued to spread the cash out thin like this, it ought to be all right. And anyway, on Claud's instructions, I'd made a point of betting a few pounds on the ringer every time he'd run, so as not to arouse any suspicion when the real day arrived. Therefore, with some confidence, I went all the way down the line staking three pounds with each book. I didn't hurry, but I didn't waste any time, either, and after each bet I wrote the amount on the back of the card before slipping it into my pocket. There were seventeen bookies. I had seventeen tickets and had laid out fifty-one pounds without disturbing the price one point. Forty-nine pounds left to get on. I glanced quickly down the hill. One owner and his dog had already reached the traps. The others were only twenty or thirty yards away. Except for Claud. Claud and Jackie were only halfway there. I could see Claud in his old khaki greatcoat sauntering slowly along with Jackie pulling ahead keenly on the leash, and once I saw him stop completely and bend down pretending to pick something up. When he went on again, he seemed to have developed a limp so as to go slower still. I hurried back to the other end of the line to start again.

"Three pounds Black Panther."

The bookmaker, the one with the magenta face and the white substance around the mouth, glanced up sharply, remembering the last time, and in one swift almost graceful movement of the arm he licked his fingers and wiped the figure twenty-five neatly off the board. His wet fingers left a small dark patch opposite Black Panther's name.

"All right, you got one more seventy-five to three," he said. "But that's the lot." Then he raised his voice and shouted, "Fifteen to one Black Panther! Fifteens the Panther!"

All down the line the twenty-fives were wiped out and it was fifteen to one the Panther now. I took it quick, but by the time I was through, the bookies had had enough and they weren't quoting him anymore. They'd only taken six pounds each, but they stood to lose a hundred and fifty, and for them—small-time bookies at a little country flapping track—that was quite enough for one race, thank you very much. I felt pleased the way I'd managed it. Lots of tickets now. I took them out of my pockets and counted them and they were like a thin pack of cards in my hand. Thirty-three tickets in all. And what did we stand to win? Let me see . . . something over two thousand pounds. Claud had said he'd win it thirty lengths. Where was Claud now?

Far away down the hill I could see the khaki greatcoat standing by the traps and the big black dog alongside. All the other dogs were already in and the owners were beginning to walk away. Claud was bending down now, coaxing Jackie into number four, and then he was closing the door and turning away and beginning to run up the hill toward the crowd, the greatcoat flapping around him. He kept looking back over his shoulder as he ran.

Beside the traps the starter stood, and his hand was up waving a handkerchief. At the other end of the track, beyond the winning post, quite close to where I stood, the man in the blue jersey was straddling the upturned bicycle on top of the wooden platform and he saw the signal and waved back and began to turn the pedals with his hands. Then a tiny white dot in the distance—the artificial hare that was in reality a football with a piece of white rabbit skin tacked on to it—began to move away from the traps, accelerating fast. The traps went up and the dogs flew out. They flew out in a single dark lump, all together, as though it were one wide dog instead of six, and almost at once I saw Jackie drawing away from the field. I knew it was Jackie because of the colour. There weren't any other black dogs in the race. It was Jackie all

right. Don't move, I told myself. Don't move a muscle or an eyelid or a toe or a fingertip. Stand quite still and don't move. Watch him going. Come on, Jackson, boy! No, don't shout. It's unlucky to shout. And don't move. Be all over in twenty seconds. Round the sharp bend now and coming up the hill and he must be fifteen or twenty lengths clear. Easy twenty lengths. Don't count the lengths, it's unlucky. And don't move. Don't move your head. Watch him out of your eye corners. Watch that Jackson go! He's really laying down to it now up that hill. He's won it now! He can't lose it now. . . .

When I got over to him, he was fighting the rabbit skin and trying to pick it up in his mouth, but his muzzle wouldn't allow it, and the other dogs were pounding up behind him and suddenly they were all on top of him grabbing for the rabbit and I got hold of him round the neck and dragged him clear, like Claud had said, and knelt down on the grass and held him tight with both arms round his body. The other catchers were having a time all trying to grab their own dogs.

Then Claud was beside me, blowing heavily, unable to speak from blowing and excitement, removing Jackie's muzzle, putting on the collar and lead, and Mr. Feasey was there too, standing with hands on hips, the button mouth pursed up tight like a mushroom, the two little cameras staring at Jackie all over again.

"So that's the game, is it?" he said.

Claud was bending over the dog and acting like he hadn't heard.

"I don't want you here no more after this, you understand that?"

Claud went on fiddling with Jackie's collar.

I heard someone behind us saying, "That flat-faced bastard with the frown swung it properly on old Feasey this time." Someone else laughed. Mr. Feasey walked away. Claud straightened up and went over with Jackie to the hare driver in the blue jersey who had dismounted from his platform.

"Cigarette," Claud said, offering the pack.

The man took one, also the five-pound note that was folded up small in Claud's fingers.

"Thanks," Claud said. "Thanks very much."

"Don't mention," the man said.

Then Claud turned to me. "You get it all on, Gordon?" He was jumping up and down and rubbing his hands and patting Jackie, and his lips trembled as he spoke.

"Yes. Half at twenty-fives, half at fifteens."

"Oh Christ, Gordon, that's marvellous. Wait here till I get the suitcase."

"You take Jackie," I said, "and go and sit in the car. I'll see you later."

There was nobody around the bookies now. I was the

only one with anything to collect, and I walked slowly, with a sort of dancing stride and a wonderful bursting feeling in my chest, toward the first one in the line, the man with the magenta face and the white substance on his mouth. I stood in front of him and I took all the time I wanted going through my pack of tickets to find the two that were his. The name was Syd Pratchett. It was written up large across his board in gold letters on a scarlet field—"SYD PRATCHETT. THE BEST ODDS IN THE MIDLANDS. PROMPT SETTLEMENT."

I handed him the first ticket and said, "Seventy-eight pounds to come." It sounded so good I said it again, making a delicious little song of it. "Seventy-eight pounds to come on this one." I didn't mean to gloat over Mr. Pratchett. As a matter of fact, I was beginning to like him quite a lot. I even felt sorry for him having to fork out so much money. I hoped his wife and kids wouldn't suffer.

"Number forty-two," Mr. Pratchett said, turning to his clerk who held the big book. "Forty-two wants seventy-eight pound."

There was a pause while the clerk ran his finger down the column of recorded bets. He did this twice; then he looked up at the boss and began to shake his head.

"No," he said. "Don't pay. That ticket backed Snailbox Lady."

Mr. Pratchett, standing on his box, leaned over and peered down at the book. He seemed to be disturbed by what the clerk had said, and there was a look of genuine concern on the huge magenta face.

That clerk is a fool, I thought, and any moment now Mr. Pratchett's going to tell him so.

But when Mr. Pratchett turned back to me, the eyes

had become narrow and hostile. "Now look, Charley," he said softly. "Don't let's have any of that. You know very well you bet Snailbox. What's the idea?"

"I bet Black Panther," I said. "Two separate bets of three pounds each at twenty-five to one. Here's the second ticket."

This time he didn't even bother to check it with the book. "You bet Snailbox, Charley," he said. "I remember you coming round." With that, he turned away from me and started wiping the names of the last race runners off his board with a wet rag. Behind him, the clerk had closed the book and was lighting himself a cigarette. I stood watching them, and I could feel the sweat beginning to break through the skin all over my body.

"Let me see the book."

Mr. Pratchett blew his nose in the wet rag and dropped it to the ground. "Look," he said, "why don't you go away and stop annoying me?"

The point was this: a bookmaker's ticket, unlike a totalizator ticket, never has anything written on it regarding the nature of your bet. This is normal practice, the same at every racetrack in the country, whether it's the Silver Ring at Newmarket, the Royal Enclosure at Ascot, or a tiny country flapping track near Oxford. All you receive is a card bearing the bookie's name and a serial number. The wager is (or should be) recorded by the bookie's clerk in his book alongside the number of the ticket, but apart from that there is no evidence at all of how you betted.

"Go on," Mr. Pratchett was saying. "Hop it."

I stepped back a pace and glanced down the long line of

bookmakers. None of them was looking my way. Each was standing motionless on his little wooden box beside his wooden placard, staring straight ahead into the crowd. I went up to the next one and presented a ticket.

"I had three pounds on Black Panther at twenty-five to one," I said firmly. "Seventy-eight pounds to come."

This man, who had a soft inflamed face, went through exactly the same routine as Mr. Pratchett, questioning his clerk, peering at the book, and giving me the same answers.

"Whatever's the matter with you?" he said quietly, speaking to me as though I were eight years old. "Trying such a silly thing as that."

This time I stepped well back. "You dirty thieving bastards!" I cried. "The whole lot of you!"

Automatically, as though they were puppets, all the heads down the line flicked round and looked at me. The expressions didn't alter. It was just the heads that moved, all seventeen of them, and seventeen pairs of cold glassy eyes looked down at me. There was not the faintest flicker of interest in any of them.

"Somebody spoke," they seemed to be saying. "We didn't hear it. It's quite a nice day today."

The crowd, sensing excitement, was beginning to move in around me. I ran back to Mr. Pratchett, right up close to him and poked him in the stomach with my finger. "You're a thief! A lousy rotten little thief!" I shouted.

The extraordinary thing was, Mr. Pratchett didn't seem to resent this at all.

"Well I never," he said. "*Look* who's talking."

Then suddenly the big face broke into a wide, froglike grin, and he looked over at the crowd and shouted, "*Look* who's talking!"

All at once, everybody started to laugh. Down the line the bookies were coming to life and turning to each other and laughing and pointing at me and shouting, "*Look* who's talking! *Look* who's talking!" The crowd began to take up the cry as well, and I stood there on the grass alongside Mr. Pratchett with this wad of tickets as thick as a pack of cards in my hand, listening to them and feeling slightly hysterical. Over the heads of the people I could see Mr. Feasey beside his blackboard already chalking up the runners for the next race; and then beyond them, far away up the top of the field, I caught sight of Claud standing by the van, waiting for me with the suitcase in his hand.

It was time to go home.

The Champion of the World

ALL DAY in between serving customers, we had been crouching over the table in the office of the filling station, preparing the raisins. They were plump and soft and swollen from being soaked in water, and when you nicked them with a razor blade the skin sprang open and the jelly stuff inside squeezed out as easily as you could wish.

But we had a hundred and ninety-six of them to do altogether and the evening was nearly upon us before we had finished.

"Don't they look marvellous!" Claud cried, rubbing his hands together hard. "What time is it, Gordon?"

"Just after five."

Through the window we could see a station wagon pulling up at the pumps with a woman at the wheel and about eight children in the back eating ice creams.

"We ought to be moving soon," Claud said. "The whole thing'll be a washout if we don't arrive before sunset, you realise that." He was getting twitchy now. His face had the same flushed and pop-eyed look it got before a dog race or when there was a date with Clarice in the evening.

We both went outside and Claud gave the woman the number of gallons she wanted. When she had gone, he remained standing in the middle of the driveway squinting anxiously up at the sun, which was now only the width of a man's hand above the line of trees along the crest of the ridge on the far side of the valley.

"All right," I said. "Lock up."

He went quickly from pump to pump, securing each nozzle in its holder with a small padlock.

"You'd better take off that yellow pullover," he said.

"Why should I?"

"You'll be shining like a bloody beacon out there in the moonlight."

"I'll be all right."

"You will not," he said. "Take it off, Gordon, please. I'll see you in three minutes." He disappeared into his caravan behind the filling station, and I went indoors and changed my yellow pullover for a blue one.

When we met again outside, Claud was dressed in a pair of black trousers and a dark-green turtleneck sweater. On his head he wore a brown cloth cap with the peak pulled down low over his eyes, and he looked like an apache actor out of a nightclub.

"What's under there?" I asked, seeing the bulge at his waistline.

He pulled up his sweater and showed me two thin but very large white cotton sacks which were bound neat and tight around his belly. "To carry the stuff," he said darkly.

"I see."

"Let's go," he said.

"I still think we ought to take the car."

"It's too risky. They'll see it parked."

"But it's over three miles up to that wood."

"Yes," he said. "And I suppose you realise we can get six months in the clink if they catch us."

"You never told me that."

"Didn't I?"

"I'm not coming," I said. "It's not worth it."

"The walk will do you good, Gordon. Come on."

It was a calm sunny evening with little wisps of brilliant white cloud hanging motionless in the sky, and the valley was cool and very quiet as the two of us began walking together along the grass verge on the side of the road that ran between the hills toward Oxford.

"You got the raisins?" Claud asked.

"They're in my pocket."

"Good," he said. "Marvellous."

Ten minutes later we turned left off the main road into a narrow lane with high hedges on either side and from now on it was all uphill.

"How many keepers are there?" I asked.

"Three."

Claud threw away a half-finished cigarette. A minute later he lit another.

"I don't usually approve of new methods," he said. "Not on this sort of a job."

"Of course."

"But by God, Gordon, I think we're onto a hot one this time."

"You do?"

"There's no question about it."

"I hope you're right."

"It'll be a milestone in the history of poaching," he said. "But don't you go telling a single soul how we've done it, you understand. Because if this ever leaked out we'd have every bloody fool in the district doing the same thing and there wouldn't be a pheasant left."

"I won't say a word."

"You ought to be very proud of yourself," he went on. "There's been men with brains studying this problem for hundreds of years and not one of them's ever come up with anything even a quarter as artful as you have. Why didn't you tell me about it before?"

"You never invited my opinion," I said.

And that was the truth. In fact, up until the day before, Claud had never even offered to discuss with me the sacred subject of poaching. Often enough, on a summer's evening when work was finished, I had seen him with cap on head sliding quietly out of his caravan and disappearing up the road towards the woods; and sometimes, watching him through the window of the filling station, I would find myself wondering exactly what he was going to do, what wily tricks he was going to practise all alone up there under the trees in the dead of night. He seldom came back until very late, and never, absolutely never, did he bring any of the spoils with him personally on his return. But the following afternoon—and I couldn't imagine how he did it—there would always be a pheasant or a hare or a brace of partridges hanging up in the shed behind the filling station for us to eat.

This summer he had been particularly active, and during the last couple of months he had stepped up the tempo to a point where he was going out four and some-

times five nights a week. But that was not all. It seemed to me that recently his whole attitude toward poaching had undergone a subtle and mysterious change. He was more purposeful about it now, more tight-lipped and intense than before, and I had the impression that this was not so much a game any longer as a crusade, a sort of private war that Claud was waging single-handed against an invisible and hated enemy.

But who?

I wasn't sure about this, but I had a suspicion that it was none other than the famous Mr. Victor Hazel himself, the owner of the land and the pheasants. Mr. Hazel was a pie and sausage manufacturer with an unbelievably arrogant manner. He was rich beyond words, and his property stretched for miles along either side of the valley. He was a self-made man with no charm at all and precious few virtues. He loathed all persons of humble station, having once been one of them himself, and he strove desperately to mingle with what he believed were the right kind of folk. He hunted with the hounds and gave shooting parties and wore fancy waistcoats, and every weekday he drove an enormous black Rolls-Royce past the filling station on his way to the factory. As he flashed by, we would sometimes catch a glimpse of the great glistening butcher's face above the wheel, pink as a ham, all soft and inflamed from eating too much meat.

Anyway, yesterday afternoon, right out of the blue, Claud had suddenly said to me, "I'll be going on up to Hazel's wood again tonight. Why don't you come along?"

"Who, me?"

"It's about the last chance this year for pheasants," he had said. "The shooting season opens Saturday and the birds'll be scattered all over the place after that—if there's any left."

"Why the sudden invitation?" I had asked, greatly suspicious.

"No special reason, Gordon. No reason at all."

"Is it risky?"

He hadn't answered this.

"I suppose you keep a gun or something hidden away up there?"

"A gun!" he cried, disgusted. "Nobody ever *shoots* pheasants, didn't you know that? You've only got to fire a *cap-pistol* in Hazel's woods and the keepers'll be on you."

"Then how do you do it?"

"Ah," he said, and the eyelids drooped over the eyes, veiled and secretive.

There was a long pause. Then he said, "Do you think you could keep your mouth shut if I was to tell you a thing or two?"

"Definitely."

"I've never told this to anyone else in my whole life, Gordon."

"I am greatly honoured," I said. "You can trust me completely."

He turned his head, fixing me with pale eyes. The eyes were large and wet and ox-like, and they were so near to me that I could see my own face reflected upside down in the centre of each.

"I am now about to let you in on the three best ways in the world of poaching a pheasant," he said. "And seeing that you're the guest on this little trip, I am going to give you the choice of which one you'd like us to use tonight. How's that?"

"There's a catch in this."

"There's no catch, Gordon. I swear it."

"All right, go on."

"Now here's the thing," he said. "Here's the first big secret." He paused and took a long suck at his cigarette. "Pheasants," he whispered softly, "is *crazy* about raisins."

"Raisins?"

"Just ordinary raisins. It's like a mania with them. My dad discovered that more than forty years ago, just like he discovered all three of these methods I'm about to describe to you now."

"I thought you said your dad was a drunk."

"Maybe he was. But he was also a great poacher, Gordon. Possibly the greatest there's ever been in the history of England. My dad studied poaching like a scientist."

"Is that so?"

"I mean it. I really mean it."

"I believe you."

"Do you know," he said, "my dad used to keep a whole flock of prime cockerels in the back yard purely for experimental purposes."

"Cockerels?"

"That's right. And whenever he thought up some new stunt for catching a pheasant, he'd try it out on a cockerel first to see how it worked. That's how he discovered about raisins. It's also how he invented the horsehair method."

Claud paused and glanced over his shoulder as though to make sure that there was nobody listening. "Here's how it's done," he said. "First you take a few raisins and you soak them overnight in water to make them nice and plump and juicy. Then you get a bit of good stiff horsehair and you cut it up into half-inch lengths. Then you push one of these lengths of horsehair through the middle of each raisin so that there's about an eighth of an inch of it sticking out on either side. You follow?"

"Yes."

"Now—the old pheasant comes along and eats one of these raisins. Right? And you're watching him from behind a tree. So what then?"

"I imagine it sticks in his throat."

"That's obvious, Gordon. But here's the amazing thing. Here's what my dad discovered. The moment this happens, the bird *never moves his feet again!* He becomes absolutely rooted to the spot, and there he stands pumping his silly neck up and down just like it was a piston, and all you've got to do is walk calmly out from the place where you're hiding and pick him up in your hands."

"I don't believe that."

"I swear it," he said. "Once a pheasant's had the horsehair, you can fire a rifle in his ear and he won't even

jump. It's just one of those unexplainable little things. But it takes a genius to discover it."

He paused, and there was a gleam of pride in his eye now as he dwelt for a moment or two upon the memory of his father, the great inventor.

"So that's Method Number One," he said. "Method Number Two is even more simple still. All you do is you have a fishing line. Then you bait the hook with a raisin and you fish for the pheasant just like you fish for a fish. You pay out the line about fifty yards and you lie there on your stomach in the bushes waiting till you get a bite. Then you haul him in."

"I don't think your father invented that one."

"It's very popular with fishermen," he said, choosing not to hear me. "Keen fishermen who can't get down to the seaside as often as they want. It gives them a bit of the old thrill. The only trouble is it's rather noisy. The pheasant squawks like hell as you haul him in, and then every keeper in the wood comes running."

"What is Method Number Three?" I asked.

"Ah," he said. "Number Three's a real beauty. It was the last one my dad ever invented before he passed away."

"His final great work?"

"Exactly, Gordon. And I can even remember the very day it happened, a Sunday morning it was, and suddenly my dad comes into the kitchen holding a huge white cockerel in his hands, and he says, 'I think I've got it.' There's a little smile on his face and a shine of glory in his eyes and he comes in very soft and quiet and he puts the bird down right in the middle of the kitchen table and he says, 'By God, I think I've got a good one this time.' 'A good what?' Mum says, looking up from the sink.

'Horace, take that filthy bird off my table.' The cockerel has a funny little paper hat over its head, like an ice-cream cone upside down, and my dad is pointing to it proudly. 'Stroke him,' he said. 'He won't move an inch.' The cockerel starts scratching away at the paper hat with one of its feet, but the hat seems to be stuck on with glue and it won't come off. 'No bird in the world is going to run away once you cover up his eyes,' my dad says, and he starts poking the cockerel with his finger and pushing it around on the table, but it doesn't take the slightest bit of notice. 'You can have this one,' he says, talking to Mum. 'You can kill it and dish it up for dinner as a celebration of what I have just invented.' And then straightaway he takes me by the arm and marches me quickly out the door, and off we go over the fields and up into the big forest the other side of Haddenham which used to belong to the Duke of Buckingham, and in less than two hours we get five lovely fat pheasants with no more trouble than it takes to go out and buy them in a shop."

Claud paused for breath. His eyes were huge and moist and dreamy as they gazed back into the wonderful world of his youth.

"I don't quite follow this," I said. "How did he get the paper hats over the pheasants' heads up in the woods?"

"You'd never guess it."

"I'm sure I wouldn't."

"Then here it is. First of all you dig a little hole in the ground. Then you twist a piece of paper into the shape of a cone and you fit this into the hole, hollow end upward, like a cup. Then you smear the paper cup all around the inside with birdlime and drop in a few raisins. At the same time, you lay a trail of raisins along the ground leading up to it. Now—the old pheasant comes pecking along the trail, and when he gets to the hole he pops his head inside to gobble the raisins and the next thing he knows he's got a paper hat stuck over his eyes and he can't see a thing. Isn't it marvellous what some people think of, Gordon? Don't you agree?"

"Your dad was a genius," I said.

"Then take your pick. Choose whichever one of the three methods you fancy and we'll use it tonight."

"You don't think they're all just a trifle on the crude side, do you?"

"Crude!" he cried, aghast. "Oh my God! And who's been having roasted pheasant in the house nearly every single day for the last six months and not a penny to pay?"

He turned and walked away toward the door of the workshop. I could see that he was deeply pained by my remark.

"Wait a minute," I said. "Don't go."

"You want to come or don't you?"

"Yes, but let me ask you something first. I've just had a bit of an idea."

"Keep it," he said. "You are talking about a subject you don't know the first thing about."

"Do you remember that bottle of sleeping pills the doc gave me last month when I had a bad back?"

"What about them?"

"Is there any reason why those wouldn't work on a pheasant?"

Claud closed his eyes and shook his head pityingly from side to side.

"Wait," I said.

"It's not worth discussing," he said. "No pheasant in the world is going to swallow those lousy red capsules. Don't you know any better than that?"

"You are forgetting the raisins," I said. "Now listen to this. We take a raisin. Then we soak it till it swells. Then we make a tiny slit in one side of it with a razor blade. Then we hollow it out a little. Then we open up one of my red capsules and pour all the powder into the raisin. Then we get a needle and cotton and very carefully we sew up the slit. Now . . ."

Out of the corner of my eye, I saw Claud's mouth slowly beginning to open.

"Now," I said. "We have a nice clean-looking raisin with two and a half grains of Seconal inside it, and let me tell *you* something now. That's enough dope to knock the average *man* unconscious, never mind about *birds!*"

I paused for ten seconds to allow the full impact of this to strike home.

"What's more, with this method we could operate on a really grand scale. We could prepare *twenty* raisins if we felt like it, and all we'd have to do is scatter them around the feeding grounds at sunset and then walk away. Half an hour later we'd come back, and the pills would be beginning to work, and the pheasants would be up in the trees by then, roosting, and they'd be starting to feel groggy, and they'd be wobbling and trying to keep their balance, and soon every pheasant that had eaten *one single raisin* would keel over unconscious and fall to the ground. My dear boy, they'd be dropping out of the trees like apples, and all we'd have to do is walk around picking them up!"

Claud was staring at me, rapt.

"Oh Christ," he said softly.

"And they'd never catch us either. We'd simply stroll through the woods dropping a few raisins here and there as we went, and even if they were *watching* us they wouldn't notice anything."

"Gordon," he said, laying a hand on my knee and gazing at me with eyes large and bright as two stars. "If this thing works, it will *revolutionise* poaching."

"I'm glad to hear it."

"How many pills have you got left?" he asked.

"Forty-nine. There were fifty in the bottle and I've only used one."

"Forty-nine's not enough. We want at least two hundred."

"Are you mad!" I cried.

He walked slowly away and stood by the door with his back to me, gazing at the sky.

"Two hundred's the bare minimum," he said quietly. "There's really not much point in doing it unless we have two hundred."

What is it now, I wondered. What the hell's he trying to do?

"This is the last chance we'll have before the season opens," he said.

"I couldn't possibly get any more."

"You wouldn't want us to come back empty-handed, would you?"

"But why so *many?*"

Claud turned his head and looked at me with large innocent eyes. "Why not?" he said gently. "Do you have any objection?"

My God, I thought suddenly. The crazy bastard is out to wreck Mr. Victor Hazel's opening-day shooting party.

"You get us two hundred of those pills," he said, "and then it'll be worth doing."

"I can't."

"You could try, couldn't you?"

Mr. Hazel's party took place on the first of October every year and it was a very famous event. Debilitated gentlemen in tweed suits, some with titles and some who were merely rich, motored in from miles around with their gunbearers and dogs and wives, and all day long the noise of shooting rolled across the valley. There were always enough pheasants to go around, for each summer the woods were methodically restocked with dozens and dozens of young birds at incredible expense. I had heard it said that the cost of rearing and keeping each pheasant up to the time when it was ready to be shot was well over five pounds (which is approximately the price of two hundred loaves of bread). But to Mr. Hazel it was worth every penny of it. He became, if only for a few hours, a big cheese in a little world and even the Lord Lieutenant of

the County slapped him on the back and tried to remember his first name when he said goodbye.

"How would it be if we just reduced the dose?" Claud asked. "Why couldn't we divide the contents of one capsule among four raisins?"

"I suppose you could if you wanted to."

"But would a quarter of a capsule be strong enough for each bird?"

One simply had to admire the man's nerve. It was dangerous enough to poach a single pheasant up in those woods at this time of year and here he was planning to knock off the bloody lot.

"A quarter would be plenty," I said.

"You're sure of that?"

"Work it out for yourself. It's all done by body weight.

You'd still be giving about twenty times more than is necessary."

"Then we'll quarter the dose," he said, rubbing his hands. He paused and calculated for a moment. "We'll have one hundred and ninety-six raisins!"

"Do you realise what that involves?" I said. "They'll take hours to prepare."

"What of it!" he cried. "We'll go tomorrow instead. We'll soak the raisins overnight and then we'll have all morning and afternoon to get them ready."

And that was precisely what we did.

Now, twenty-four hours later, we were on our way. We had been walking steadily for about forty minutes and we were nearing the point where the lane curved around to the right and ran along the crest of the hill toward the big wood where the pheasants lived. There was about a mile to go.

"I don't suppose by any chance these keepers might be carrying guns?" I asked.

"All keepers carry guns," Claud said.

I had been afraid of that.

"It's for the vermin mostly."

"Ah."

"Of course there's no guarantee they won't take a pot at a poacher now and again."

"You're joking."

"Not at all. But they only do it from behind. Only when you're running away. They like to pepper you in the legs at about fifty yards."

"They can't do that!" I cried. "It's a criminal offence!"

"So is poaching," Claud said.

We walked on awhile in silence. The sun was below the

high hedge on our right now and the lane was in shadow.

"You consider yourself lucky this isn't thirty years ago," he went on. "They used to shoot you on sight in those days."

"Do you believe that?"

"I know it," he said. "Many's the night when I was a nipper I've gone into the kitchen and seen my old dad lying face downward on the table and Mum standing over him digging the grapeshot out of his buttocks with a potato knife."

"Stop," I said. "It makes me nervous."

"You believe me, don't you?"

"Yes, I believe you."

"Toward the end he was so covered in tiny little white scars he looked exactly like it was snowing."

"Yes," I said. "All right."

" 'Poacher's arse,' they used to call it," Claud said. "And there wasn't a man in the whole village who didn't have a bit of it one way or another. But my dad was the champion."

"Good luck to him," I said.

"I wish to hell he was here now," Claud said, wistful. "He'd have given anything in the world to be coming with us on this job tonight."

"He could take my place," I said. "Gladly."

We had reached the crest of the hill and now we could see the wood ahead of us, huge and dark with the sun going down behind the trees and little sparks of gold shining through.

"You'd better let me have those raisins," Claud said.

I gave him the bag and he slid it gently into his trouser pocket.

"No talking once we're inside," he said. "Just follow me and try not to go snapping any branches."

Five minutes later we were there. The lane ran right up to the wood itself and then skirted the edge of it for about three hundred yards with only a little hedge between. Claud slipped through the hedge on all fours and I followed.

It was cool and dark inside the wood. No sunlight came in at all.

"This is spooky," I said.

"Ssshh!"

Claud was very tense. He was walking just ahead of me, picking his feet up high and putting them down gently on the moist ground. He kept his head moving all the time, the eyes sweeping slowly from side to side, searching for danger. I tried doing the same, but soon I began to see a keeper behind every tree, so I gave up.

Then a large patch of sky appeared ahead of us in the roof of the forest and I knew that this must be the clearing. Claud had told me that the clearing was the place where the young birds were introduced into the woods in early July, where they were fed and watered and guarded by the keepers, and where many of them stayed from force of habit until the shooting began.

"There's always plenty of pheasants in the clearing," he had said.

"Keepers too, I suppose."

"Yes, but there's thick bushes all around, and that helps."

We were now advancing in a series of quick crouching spurts, running from tree to tree and stopping and waiting and listening and running on again, and then at last

we were kneeling safely behind a big clump of alder right on the edge of the clearing and Claud was grinning and nudging me in the ribs and pointing through the branches at the pheasants.

The place was absolutely stiff with birds. There must have been two hundred of them, at least, strutting around among the tree stumps.

"You see what I mean?" Claud whispered.

It was an astonishing sight, a sort of poacher's dream come true. And how close they were! Some of them were not more than ten paces from where we knelt. The hens were plump and creamy-brown and they were so fat their breast feathers almost brushed the ground as they walked. The cocks were slim and beautiful, with long tails and brilliant red patches around the eyes, like scarlet spectacles. I glanced at Claud. His big ox-like face was transfixed in ecstasy. The mouth was slightly open and the eyes had a kind of glazy look about them as they stared at the pheasants.

I believe that all poachers react in roughly the same way as this on sighting game. They are like women who sight large emeralds in a jeweller's window, the only difference being that the women are less dignified in the methods they employ later on to acquire the loot. Poacher's arse is nothing to the punishment that a female is willing to endure.

"Aha," Claud said softly. "You see the keeper?"

"Where?"

"Over the other side, by that big tree. Look carefully."

"My God!"

"It's all right. He can't see *us.*"

We crouched close to the ground, watching the keeper. He was a smallish man with a cap on his head and a gun under his arm. He never moved. He was like a little post standing there.

"Let's go," I whispered.

The keeper's face was shadowed by the peak of his cap, but it seemed to me that he was looking directly at us.

"I'm not staying here," I said.

"Hush," Claud said.

Slowly, never taking his eyes from the keeper, he reached into his pocket and brought out a single raisin. He placed it in the palm of his right hand, and then quickly, with a little flick of the wrist, he threw the raisin high into the air. I watched it as it went sailing over the bushes and I saw it land within a yard or so of two henbirds standing together beside an old tree stump. Both birds turned their heads sharply at the drop of the raisin. Then one of them hopped over and made a quick peck at the ground and that must have been it.

I glanced up at the keeper. He hadn't moved.

Claud threw a second raisin into the clearing; then a third, and a fourth, and a fifth.

At this point, I saw the keeper turn away his head in order to survey the wood behind him.

Quick as a flash, Claud pulled the paper bag out of his pocket and tipped a huge pile of raisins into the cup of his right hand.

"Stop," I said.

But with a great sweep of the arm he flung the whole handful high over the bushes into the clearing.

They fell with a soft little patter, like raindrops on dry leaves, and every single pheasant in the place must either have seen them coming or heard them fall. There was a flurry of wings and a rush to find the treasure.

The keeper's head flicked round as though there were a spring inside his neck. The birds were all pecking away madly at the raisins. The keeper took two quick paces forward and for a moment I thought he was going in to investigate. But then he stopped, and his face came up and his eyes began travelling slowly around the perimeter of the clearing.

"Follow me," Claud whispered. "And *keep down.*" He started crawling away swiftly on all fours, like some kind of a monkey.

I went after him. He had his nose close to the ground and his huge tight buttocks were winking at the sky, and it was easy to see now how poacher's arse had come to be an occupational disease among the fraternity.

We went along like this for about a hundred yards.

"Now run," Claud said.

We got to our feet and ran, and a few minutes later we emerged through the hedge into the lovely open safety of the lane.

"It went marvellous," Claud said, breathing heavily. "Didn't it go absolutely marvellous?" The big face was scarlet and glowing with triumph.

"It was a mess," I said.

"What!" he cried.

"Of course it was. We can't possibly go back now. That keeper knows there was someone there."

"He knows nothing," Claud said. "In another five minutes it'll be pitch dark inside the wood and he'll be sloping off home to his supper."

"I think I'll join him."

"You're a great poacher," Claud said. He sat down on the grassy bank under the hedge and lit a cigarette.

The sun had set now and the sky was a pale smoke blue, faintly glazed with yellow. In the wood behind us the shadows and the spaces in between the trees were turning from grey to black.

"How long does a sleeping pill take to work?" Claud asked.

"Look out," I said. "There's someone coming."

The man had appeared suddenly and silently out of the dusk and he was only thirty yards away when I saw him.

"Another bloody keeper," Claud said.

We both looked at the keeper as he came down the lane toward us. He had a shotgun under his arm and there

was a black Labrador walking at his heels. He stopped when he was a few paces away and the dog stopped with him and stayed behind him, watching us through the keeper's legs.

"Good evening," Claud said, nice and friendly.

This one was a tall bony man, about forty, with a swift eye and a hard cheek and hard dangerous hands.

"I know you," he said softly, coming closer. "I know the both of you."

Claud didn't answer this.

"You're from the fillin' station. Right?"

His lips were thin and dry, with some sort of a brownish crust over them.

"You're Cubbage and Hawes, and you're from the fillin' station on the main road. Right?"

"What are we playing?" Claud said. "Twenty Questions?"

The keeper spat out a big gob of spit and I saw it go floating through the air and land with a plop on a patch of dry dust six inches from Claud's feet. It looked like a little baby oyster lying there.

"Beat it," the man said. "Go on. Get out."

Claud sat on the bank smoking his cigarette and looking at the gob of spit.

"Go on," the man said. "Get out."

When he spoke, the upper lip lifted above the gum and I could see a row of small discoloured teeth, one of them black, the others quince and ochre.

"This happens to be a public highway," Claud said. "Kindly do not molest us."

The keeper shifted the gun from his left arm to his right.

"You're loiterin'," he said, "with intent to commit a felony. I could run you in for that."

"No, you couldn't," Claud said.

All this made me rather nervous.

"I've had my eye on you for some time," the keeper said, looking at Claud.

"It's getting late," I said. "Shall we stroll on?"

Claud flipped away his cigarette and got slowly to his feet. "All right," he said. "Let's go."

We wandered off down the lane the way we had come, leaving the keeper standing there, and soon the man was out of sight in the half-darkness behind us.

"That's the head keeper," Claud said. "His name is Rabbetts."

"Let's get the hell out," I said.

"Come in here," Claud said.

There was a gate on our left leading into a field and we climbed over it and sat down behind the hedge.

"Mr. Rabbetts is also due for his supper," Claud said. "You mustn't worry about him."

We sat quietly behind the hedge waiting for the keeper to walk past us on his way home. A few stars were showing and a bright three-quarter moon was coming up over the hills behind us in the east.

"Here he is," Claud whispered. "Don't move."

The keeper came loping softly up the lane with the dog padding quick and soft-footed at his heels, and we watched them through the hedge as they went by.

"He won't be coming back tonight," Claud said.

"How do you know that?"

"A keeper never waits for you in the wood if he knows where you live. He goes to your house and hides outside and watches for you to come back."

"That's worse."

"No, it isn't, not if you dump the loot somewhere else before you go home. He can't touch you then."

"What about the other one, the one in the clearing?"

"He's gone too."

"You can't be sure of that."

"I've been studying these bastards for months, Gordon, honest I have. I know all their habits. There's no danger."

Reluctantly I followed him back into the wood. It was

pitch dark in there now and very silent, and as we moved cautiously forward the noise of our footsteps seemed to go echoing around the walls of the forest as though we were walking in a cathedral.

"Here's where we threw the raisins," Claud said.

I peered through the bushes. The clearing lay dim and milky in the moonlight.

"You're quite sure the keeper's gone?"

"I *know* he's gone."

I could just see Claud's face under the peak of his cap, the pale lips, the soft pale cheeks, and the large eyes with a little spark of excitement dancing slowly in each.

"Are they roosting?"

"Yes."

"Whereabouts?"

"All around. They don't go far."

"What do we do next?"

"We stay here and wait. I brought you a light," he added, and he handed me one of those small pocket flashlights shaped like a fountain pen. "You may need it."

I was beginning to feel better. "Shall we see if we can spot some of them sitting in the trees?" I said.

"No."

"I should like to see how they look when they're roosting."

"This isn't a nature study," Claud said. "Please be quiet."

We stood there for a long time waiting for something to happen.

"I've just had a nasty thought," I said. "If a bird can

keep its balance on a branch when it's asleep, then surely there isn't any reason why the pills should make it fall down."

Claud looked at me quick.

"After all," I said, "it's not dead. It's still only sleeping."

"It's doped," Claud said.

"But that's just a *deeper* sort of sleep. Why should we expect it to fall down just because it's in a *deeper* sleep?"

There was a gloomy silence.

"We should've tried it with chickens," Claud said. "My dad would've done that."

"Your dad was a genius," I said.

At that moment, there came a soft thump from the wood behind us.

"Hey!"

"Ssshh!"

We stood listening.

Thump.

"There's another!"

It was a deep muffled sound, as though a bag of sand had been dropped from about shoulder height.

Thump!

"They're pheasants!" I cried.

"Wait!"

"I'm sure they're pheasants!"

Thump! Thump!

"You're right!"

We ran back into the wood.

"Where were they?"

"Over here! Two of them were over here!"

"I thought they were this way."

"Keep looking!" Claud shouted. "They can't be far."

We searched for about a minute.

"Here's one!" he called.

When I got to him, he was holding a magnificent cockbird in both hands. We examined it closely with our flashlights.

"It's doped to the gills," Claud said. "It's still alive, I can feel its heart, but it's doped to the bloody gills."

Thump!

"There's another!"

Thump! Thump!

"Two more!"

Thump!

Thump! Thump! Thump!

"Jesus Christ!"

Thump! Thump! Thump! Thump!

Thump! Thump!

All around us the pheasants were starting to rain down out of the trees. We began rushing around madly in the dark, sweeping the ground with our flashlights.

Thump! Thump! Thump! This lot fell almost on top of me. I was right under the tree as they came down and I found all three of them immediately—two cocks and a hen. They were limp and warm, the feathers wonderfully soft in the hand.

"Where shall I put them?" I called out. I was holding them by the legs.

"Lay them here, Gordon! Just pile them up here where it's light!"

Claud was standing on the edge of the clearing with the moonlight streaming down all over him and a great bunch of pheasants in each hand. His face was bright, his

eyes big and bright and wonderful, and he was staring around him like a child who has just discovered that the whole world is made of chocolate.

Thump!

Thump! Thump!

"I don't like it," I said. "It's too many."

"It's beautiful!" he cried, and he dumped the birds he was carrying and ran off to look for more.

Thump! Thump! Thump! Thump!

Thump!

It was easy to find them now. There were one or two lying under every tree. I quickly collected six more, three in each hand, and ran back and dumped them with the others. Then six more. Then six more after that.

And still they kept falling.

Claud was in a whirl of ecstasy now, dashing about like a mad ghost under the trees. I could see the beam of his flashlight waving around in the dark and each time he found a bird he gave a little yelp of triumph.

Thump! Thump! Thump!

"That bugger Hazel ought to hear this!" he called out.

"Don't shout," I said. "It frightens me."

"What's that?"

"Don't *shout.* There might be keepers."

"Screw the keepers!" he cried. "They're all eating!"

For three or four minutes, the pheasant kept on falling. Then suddenly they stopped.

"Keep searching!" Claud shouted. "There's plenty more on the ground!"

"Don't you think we ought to get out while the going's good?"

"No," he said.

We went on searching. Between us we looked under every tree within a hundred yards of the clearing, north, south, east, and west, and I think we found most of them in the end. At the collecting point there was a pile of pheasants as big as a bonfire.

"It's a miracle," Claud was saying. "It's a bloody miracle." He was staring at them in a kind of trance.

"We'd better just take half a dozen each and get out quick," I said.

"I would like to count them, Gordon."

"There's no time for that."

"I must count them."

"No," I said. "Come on."

"One . . .

"Two . . .

"Three . . .

"Four . . ."

He began counting them very carefully, picking up each bird in turn and laying it carefully to one side. The moon was directly overhead now and the whole clearing was brilliantly illuminated.

"I'm not standing around here like this," I said. I walked back a few paces and hid myself in the shadows, waiting for him to finish.

"A hundred and seventeen . . . a hundred and eighteen . . . a hundred and nineteen . . . *a hundred and twenty!*" he cried. "*One hundred and twenty birds!* It's an all-time record!"

I didn't doubt it for a moment.

"The most my dad ever got in one night was fifteen and he was drunk for a week afterwards!"

"You're the champion of the world," I said. "Are you ready now?"

"One minute," he answered, and he pulled up his sweater and proceeded to unwind the two big white cotton sacks from around his belly. "Here's yours," he said, handing one of them to me. "Fill it up quick."

The light of the moon was so strong I could read the small print along the base of the sack. "J. W. Crump," it said. "Keston Flour Mills, London SW17."

"You don't think that bastard with the brown teeth is watching us this very moment from behind a tree?"

"There's no chance of that," Claud said. "He's down at the filling station like I told you, waiting for us to come home."

We started loading the pheasants into the sacks. They were soft and floppy-necked and the skin underneath the feathers was still warm.

"There'll be a taxi waiting for us in the lane," Claud said.

"What?"

"I always go back in a taxi, Gordon, didn't you know that?"

I told him I didn't.

"A taxi is anonymous," Claud said. "Nobody knows who's inside a taxi except the driver. My dad taught me that."

"Which driver?"

"Charlie Kinch. He's only too glad to oblige."

We finished loading the pheasants and then we humped the sacks onto our shoulders and started staggering through the pitch-black wood toward the lane.

"I'm not walking all the way back to the village with

this," I said. My sack had sixty birds inside it and it must have weighed a hundredweight and a half at least.

"Charlie's never let me down yet," Claud said.

We came to the margin of the wood and peered through the hedge into the lane. Claud said, "Charlie boy," very softly, and the old man behind the wheel of the taxi not five yards away poked his head out into the moonlight and gave us a sly toothless grin. We slid through the hedge, dragging the sacks after us along the ground.

"Hullo!" Charlie said. "What's this?"

"It's cabbages," Claud told him. "Open the door."

Two minutes later we were safely inside the taxi, cruising slowly down the hill toward the village.

It was all over now bar the shouting. Claud was triumphant, bursting with pride and excitement, and he kept leaning forward and tapping Charlie Kinch on the shoulder and saying, "How about it, Charlie? How about this for a haul?" and Charlie kept glancing back pop-eyed at the huge bulging sacks lying on the floor between us and saying, "Jesus Christ, man, how did you do it?"

"There's six brace of them for you, Charlie," Claud said. And Charlie said, "I reckon pheasants is going to be a bit scarce up at Mr. Victor Hazel's opening-day shoot this year," and Claud said, "I imagine they are, Charlie, I imagine they are."

"What in God's name are you going to do with a hundred and twenty pheasants?" I asked.

"Put them in cold storage for the winter," Claud said. "Put them in with the dogmeat in the deep freeze at the filling station."

"Not tonight, I trust?"

"No, Gordon, not tonight. We leave them at Bessie's house tonight."

"Bessie who?"

"Bessie Organ."

"Bessie *Organ!*"

"Bessie always delivers my game, didn't you know that?"

"I don't know anything," I said. I was completely stunned. Mrs. Organ was the wife of the Reverend Jack Organ, the local vicar.

"Always choose a respectable woman to deliver your game," Claud announced. "That's correct, Charlie, isn't it?"

"Bessie's a right smart girl," Charlie said.

We were driving through the village now and the streetlamps were still on and the men were wandering home from the pubs. I saw Will Prattley letting himself in quietly by the side door of his fishmonger's shop and Mrs. Prattley's head was sticking out the window just above him, but he didn't know it.

"The vicar is very partial to roasted pheasant," Claud said.

"He hangs it eighteen days," Charlie said; "then he gives it a couple of good shakes and all the feathers drop off."

The taxi turned left and swung in through the gates of the vicarage. There were no lights on in the house and nobody met us. Claud and I dumped the pheasants in the coal shed at the rear, and then we said goodbye to Charlie Kinch and walked back in the moonlight to the filling station, empty-handed. Whether or not Mr. Rabbetts was watching us as we went in, I do not know. We saw no sign of him.

"Here she comes," Claud said to me the next morning.

"Who?"

"Bessie—Bessie Organ." He spoke the name proudly and with a slight proprietary air, as though he were a general referring to his bravest officer.

I followed him outside.

"Down there," he said, pointing.

Far away down the road I could see a small female figure advancing toward us.

"What's she pushing?" I asked.

Claud gave me a sly look.

"There's only one safe way of delivering game," he announced, "and that's under a baby."

"Yes," I murmured, "yes, of course."

"That'll be young Christopher Organ in there, aged one and a half. He's a lovely child, Gordon."

I could just make out the small dot of a baby sitting high up in the pram, which had its hood folded down.

"There's sixty or seventy pheasants at least under that little nipper," Claud said happily. "You just imagine that."

"You can't put sixty or seventy pheasants in a pram."

"You can if it's got a good deep well underneath it, and if you take out the mattress and pack them in tight, right up to the top. All you need then is a sheet. You'll be surprised how little room a pheasant takes up when it's limp."

We stood beside the pumps waiting for Bessie Organ to arrive. It was one of those warm windless September mornings with a darkening sky and a smell of thunder in the air.

"Right through the village bold as brass," Claud said. "Good old Bessie."

"She seems in rather a hurry to me."

Claud lit a new cigarette from the stub of the old one. "Bessie is never in a hurry," he said.

"She certainly isn't walking normal," I told him. "You look."

He squinted at her through the smoke of his cigarette. Then he took the cigarette out of his mouth and looked again.

"Well?" I said.

"She does seem to be going a tiny bit quick, doesn't she?" he said carefully.

"She's going damn quick."

There was a pause. Claud was beginning to stare very hard at the approaching woman.

"Perhaps she doesn't want to be caught in the rain, Gordon. I'll bet that's exactly what it is, she thinks it's going to rain and she don't want the baby to get wet."

"Why doesn't she put the hood up?"

He didn't answer this.

"She's *running!*" I cried. "Look!" Bessie had suddenly broken into a full sprint.

Claud stood very still, watching the woman, and in the silence that followed I fancied I could hear a baby screaming.

"What's up?"

He didn't answer.

"There's something wrong with that baby," I said. "Listen."

At this point, Bessie was about two hundred yards away from us but closing fast.

"Can you hear him now?" I said.

"Yes."

"He's yelling his head off."

The small shrill voice in the distance was growing louder every second, frantic, piercing, nonstop, almost hysterical.

"He's having a fit," Claud announced.

"I think he must be."

"That's why she's running, Gordon. She wants to get him in here quick and put him under a cold tap."

"I'm sure you're right," I said. "In fact, I know you're right. Just listen to that noise."

"If it isn't a fit, you can bet your life it's something like it."

"I quite agree."

Claud shifted his feet uneasily on the gravel of the driveway. "There's a thousand and one different things keep happening every day to little babies like that," he said.

"Of course."

"I knew a baby once who caught his fingers in the spokes of the pram wheel. He lost the lot. It cut them clean off."

"Yes."

"Whatever it is," Claud said, "I wish to Christ she'd stop running."

A long truck loaded with bricks came up behind Bessie and the driver slowed down and poked his head out the window to stare. Bessie ignored him and flew on, and she was so close now I could see her big red face with the mouth wide open, panting for breath. I noticed she was wearing white gloves on her hands, very prim and dainty, and there was a funny little white hat to match perched right on the top of her head, like a mushroom.

Suddenly, out of the pram, straight up into the air, flew an enormous pheasant!

Claud let out a cry of horror.

The fool in the truck going along beside Bessie started roaring with laughter.

The pheasant flapped around drunkenly for a few seconds; then it lost height and landed in the grass by the side of the road.

A grocer's van came up behind the truck and began hooting to get by. Bessie kept on running.

Then—*whoosh*—a second pheasant flew up out of the pram.

Then a third, and a fourth. Then a fifth.

"My God!" I said. "It's the pills! They're wearing off!"

Claud didn't say anything.

Bessie covered the last fifty yards at a tremendous pace, and she came swinging into the driveway of the filling station with birds flying up out of the pram in all directions.

"What the hell's going on?" she cried.

"Go round the back!" I shouted. "Go round the back!" But she pulled up sharp against the first pump in the line and before we could reach her she had seized the screaming infant in her arms and dragged him clear.

"No! No!" Claud cried, racing towards her. "Don't lift the baby! Put him back! Hold down the sheet!" But she wasn't even listening, and with the weight of the child suddenly lifted away, a great cloud of pheasants rose up out of the pram, fifty or sixty of them, at least, and the whole sky above us was filled with huge brown birds clapping their wings furiously to gain height.

Claud and I started running up and down the driveway waving our arms to frighten them off the premises.

"Go away!" we shouted. "Shoo! Go away!" But they were too dopey still to take any notice of us, and within half a minute down they came again and settled themselves like a swarm of locusts all over the front of my filling station. The place was covered with them. They sat wing to wing along the edges of the roof and on the concrete canopy that came out over the pumps, and a dozen at least were clinging to the sill of the office window. Some had flown down onto the rack that held the bottles of lubricating oil, and others were sliding about on the bonnets of my secondhand cars. One cockbird with a fine tail was perched superbly on top of a petrol pump, and quite a number, those that were too drunk to stay aloft, simply squatted in the driveway at our feet, fluffing their feathers and blinking their small eyes.

Across the road, a line of cars had already started forming behind the brick lorry and the grocery van, and people were opening their doors and getting out and beginning to cross over to have a closer look. I glanced at my watch. It was twenty to nine. Any moment now, I thought, a large black car is going to come streaking along the road from the direction of the village, and the car will be a Rolls, and the face behind the wheel will be the great glistening butcher's face of Mr. Victor Hazel, maker of sausages and pies.

"They near pecked him to pieces!" Bessie was shouting, clasping the screaming baby to her bosom.

"You go on home, Bessie," Claud said, white in the face.

"Lock up," I said. "Put out the sign. We've gone for the day."

A NOTE ON THE TYPE

This book was set in a typeface called Walbaum. The original cutting of this face was made by Justus Erich Walbaum (1768–1839) in Weimar in 1810. The type was revived by the Monotype Corporation in 1934. Young Walbaum began his artistic career as an apprentice to a maker of cookie molds. How he managed to leave this field and become a successful punch cutter remains a mystery. Although the type that bears his name may be classified as modern, numerous slight irregularities in its cut give this face its humane manner.

Composed by The Sarabande Press,
New York, New York

Printed and bound by R.R. Donnelley & Sons,
Harrisonburg, Virginia

Designed by Dorothy S. Baker